Destination Christmas, Next Stop Love

BARBARA WINKES

For D.

Chapter One

The night before Thanksgiving, Sabrina dreamed about the train again. She was five years old, holding her parents' hands as they walked up to the car. The old-fashioned train looked wondrous from the outside, its windows lit up. When they boarded and found their cabin, Sabrina couldn't believe her eyes. Everything shimmered and shone, wherever she looked, lights, Christmas ornaments and garlands.

They took their seats, Sabrina by the window, her mom next to her. Her dad sat down across from them.

The whistle made her jump, and then the doors closed with a bang. Her heart started beating faster.

They soon left the town behind for snow-covered fields and forests. Every once in a while, she saw the lights of decorated houses and trees along the way, and other villages in the distance.

"Isn't it magic?" her mother said. She and Sabrina's father shared a smile as a young woman in a pretty, dark blue uniform arrived.

"Would you like something to drink? Eggnog maybe? And a hot chocolate for the young lady?"

"That sounds wonderful. My husband and I will have the eggnog, and I think Sabrina has been waiting for that hot chocolate all day..."

"Yes!" she confirmed with all the enthusiasm of a young child about to get a sweet treat.

The ride went on, and a few minutes later, the woman returned with their orders on a tray, including a small plate of cookies. Sabrina eagerly reached for her cup. The scent of chocolate and the whipped cream on top promised a delicious treat.

The train's whistle sounded again, a different sound this time, jarring and annoying...

Blindly, Sabrina fumbled for her alarm clock, and it fell to the floor, still ringing. She got out of bed and picked up the offending object, cursing all the way.

Next, she went into the kitchen and prepared the coffeemaker before heading for the shower. She tried to clear her mind from the bittersweet ambience of the dream still lingering in reality.

Sabrina was thousands of miles away from the snow-covered hills of Boxwood, and her parents had passed away before they could see her rise to fame...and her fall.

Maybe that was too big a word. No one had called to un-invite her from the studio's Christmas party yet, but the message was clear.

Her project, in which she had invested all her heart and most of her savings, wouldn't come to pass. She had mortgaged her condo to make the movie about a woman her age finding love with another woman during the holidays, but it wouldn't see the light of day. Her mind was still reeling, disappointment and denial warring.

No wonder she kept having that dream, a means for her mind to escape.

The train ride she'd gone on with her parents every year as a child wasn't even that long, five stops, about an hour. In her mind, it had always seemed longer, and beyond magic.

Parents would tell their children that Santa needed that time so he could deliver presents to every house. Sabrina would come home so excited she thought she'd be awake all night—only to fall asleep the moment her head hit the pillow.

It always snowed in Boxwood around Christmas time.

She hadn't seen any real snow, or been back home, in a long time.

There was nothing and no one waiting there for her.

Sabrina had always enjoyed the comforts a big city had to offer. She didn't know how to deal with this latest blow. After her first successes, she had all of a sudden found herself with many friends, only to realize that most of them wanted a place in the sun next to a famous person. Often, she'd come to that conclusion too late, and now she was experiencing how fragile and fleeting that fame could be.

As she sipped her coffee in her breakfast nook, Sabrina couldn't deny reality any longer: She was beyond lonely, but there was nothing she could do about it in the near future. She had to pick herself up and continue.

She couldn't even go and visit her childhood home for sheer nostalgia. She had to sell it after her parents passed away, and a young couple with a baby had moved in. Sabrina wasn't sure if anyone still remembered her, or cared, for anything other than what they knew from her movies.

If there was something Sabrina knew she couldn't handle another disappointment.

That didn't stop her from wondering if the children of Box-wood still experienced the magic of the Christmas train. The company surely had a website by now.

Scrolling through the pages on her phone, Sabrina was immediately bombarded by Black Friday offers. A lot of people had better be buying and streaming her movies, otherwise she wouldn't be invited to the next Christmas party.

She couldn't find any information on the train which wasn't too surprising. Everything was a little more old-fashioned in Boxwood. However, the little town she'd grown up in now had a website, trying to get tourists to take a chance on their rather limited accommodations.

Sabrina gave up for the moment. It wasn't important. She wasn't going back, ever.

·♥·♥·♥·♥·♥·

The holidays were always a difficult time, Christmas especially, but Sabrina didn't want to think about it yet. She had a party to get through.

"What do you think?" she asked her stylist who regarded her with a proud gaze. She had reason to be proud, a miracle worker, in Sabrina's opinion. The golden dress might be a little too much, but she had to make an impression, think beyond the recent failure.

Before she got the sobering news, Sabrina had auditioned for a movie. She thought she'd done a decent job, though she might have turned it down had the studio gone ahead with her own project, *Love for Christmas.*

The Stranger Next Door was a romantic suspense that would pair her with a slightly older, world-famous male actor.

Sabrina would have preferred to get distribution for her own project, but that wasn't going to happen now. After facing her financial reality, she knew she needed that movie. She had worked on a somewhat regular basis since her early successes, most notably a movie called *Dreams of Gold* that got a lot of teenagers interested in ice skating.

For years now, she had hoped to achieve that kind of recognition again. She was known, famous even. The projects she'd signed up for, hadn't flopped, but they hadn't brought in the big bucks either.

Sabrina hoped her appearance tonight would make sure the right people got back to her in time. She was lucky to have a Plan B. *The Stranger Next Door* could put her back on the map in a big way.

"You look stunning."

"Thank you. That's mostly because of your skills."

Dina shook her head. "I barely did anything."

Sabrina had come to a point in her life where she wasn't sure if this was harmless flattery, or if Dina just wanted to keep her job. Either way, life would soon turn around for her. She'd make it through another set of lonely holidays and start off the year with something amazing.

This party might come with annoying but necessary small talk, but it would be worth it. No more dreaming about the unreachable. That movie was within reach, a realistic project.

Half an hour later, Sabrina stepped out of the limousine and made her way past the crowd to the hotel entrance. A quick sideways look assured her that many of the fans, and some of the paparazzi were here for her. She waved to a group of women excited to see her. For them, she would have loved to realize her project, but it wasn't meant to be. She had to secure her role in *The Stranger Next Door* first, build a better foundation for herself before rocking the boat again.

It would all happen in time.

Inside, she found the rooms where the studio held the party, admiring the tall Christmas trees on the way. Sabrina made some small talk, accepted a glass of champagne from a waiter, and finally arrived on the other side of the room where the casting director stood by the scrumptious buffet. Good. That meant she could approach him without being too obvious.

Marc was still in a conversation with a director, so she studied her options. If she didn't get anything to eat, someone might write about how she had a problem. If she loaded her plate like most of the men did in here, someone might write about how she had a problem.

"Sabrina, hi. I'm so glad you're here." She turned around to smile at her agent Marc Pearson. "Despite all," he added. "Let's drown our sorrow together?"

"Wait, why?" What had she missed?

His sympathetic gaze worried her.

"Tell me more?"

"You mean they didn't call you yet? Oh sweetie, I'm really sorry. I thought you were fabulous, but...Don't tell anyone I told you already."

"Told me what?" she asked with a frown. "I thought that was a done deal."

"It pretty much was until you miscalculated your political capital, I guess."

"It was a holiday romance! There was nothing political about it."

He shrugged. "I guess some people saw it differently."

"What does that mean? It's not like I was the first to ever suggest this. There have been TV movies, shows, streaming..."

"Well, it was suggested to me that it would be better to go with someone less...controversial."

Sabrina set down the glass right before it was about to slip from her fingers. This couldn't be.

"I don't understand. Less controversial? Who would that be?"

"Emily Davis." His quick answer told her that the decision had been made, and there was nothing Sabrina, or anyone, could do about it. She would have liked to say many things, and held back all of them, because she knew there'd be no point.

When she first started talking about *Love for Christmas*, a lot of people had encouraged her, said that it was overdue. Everyone was getting more inclusive these days. When the time came to step up, and pay up, many of the same people were reluctant to return her calls.

Maybe next time...

People aren't ready unless you have big names and big funding...

But deep down, Sabrina knew that her passion project wasn't the only thing to cost her this opportunity. She had no negative feelings for Emily who had made it part of her brand to stay away from all politics. Like Sabrina, she had to watch her every step in the public, around people, around food. Emily Davis was almost a decade younger than her.

"Okay. Wow. I see. Can't have a forty-two-year-old woman be the love interest of a forty-eight-year-old guy."

He looked embarrassed. "Again, I'm really sorry. I know many folks on the project who would have loved to work with you, but it seems the people in charge are a bit more conservative than we thought. There will always be those who want to turn back the clock."

She had almost turned down that movie. Now, it was out of her hands. Was the universe trying to tell her something?

"Come on, let's have a drink."

Sabrina shook her head. "No, thank you. I can't stay."

"I hope that wasn't because...You're going to get something else in no time. I promise you."

7

"Sure. Don't worry."

She turned around and went to get her coat from the wardrobe, then left the hotel through a side entrance. No crying. She wasn't going to ruin her make-up.

Sabrina walked down a decorated street, passing by a Santa, who, at a closer look, was raising money for an LGBTQ organization. A few steps past, she stopped and took out her wallet only to realize she didn't have any cash on her.

"I'm sorry," she mumbled, self-conscious, and kept walking. Perhaps she could come back another day, and make up for yet another mistake?

On the corner, a diner tried to attract customers with a twenty-four-hour breakfast. For the lack of anything better to do, Sabrina went inside and was about to order a coffee when she saw hot chocolate on the menu written on a blackboard behind the counter. Nothing could ever be as good as the memory of her childhood days, but she was feeling wistful and a little sorry for herself. She didn't want to drink either.

The waitress seemed rather unimpressed when she took her order, or perhaps she hadn't recognized Sabrina. Neither interpretation was improving Sabrina's mood.

"One hot chocolate, coming right up. Is there anything else I can get you?"

"No thanks."

She found a place by the window and leaned back into the booth, wondering what to do next. Tonight, and the rest of her life. She had come to the City of Angels full of hope, and the first few years seemed to tell her she was on her way. Then—what happened? She had gotten ahead of herself, in denial of how powerful the forces she was up against, were? In her peer group, people had expected her to stay polite and patient. She had made a name for herself, but not big enough to be able to make waves without consequences.

Sabrina would have loved to go home, but she wasn't sure where that was.

The waitress brought her hot chocolate, and, to her surprise, a brownie on a small Christmas plate.

"I'm sorry, I know you said...just in case you need something sweet."

"Thank you," she said, feeling a smile chasing away the frown on her face. "I thought your hot chocolate was already sweet."

"I swear I won't tell anyone."

"It's fine. Thank you. But I think I'll take this to go."

"I'll get it ready for you. And I wanted to say, it's too bad we won't get to see your holiday movie. Thank you for trying. It means a lot to many of us."

She had held it together pretty well so far, but this small act of kindness threatened her composure. Sabrina quickly took a sip, and it was almost a shock to be transported right back into her dream.

She would have to remember this place—it was as close to the real thing as she'd ever get, minus the complete comfort and safety the holidays had represented for her then.

Chapter Two

Santa had left when she walked back the same street later, and Sabrina had no choice but to take the brownie with her. It would make a tasty breakfast, at least. For what it was worth, she wouldn't wake up with a hangover—or any more illusions.

She needed a plan.

Something.

Back in her condo, she couldn't shake the feeling that there was something urgent she needed to do. But where could she go from here? Tomorrow, or any day after that, the world would learn that the role had gone to Emily. She would have to answer even more questions, to her fans, the people she hoped would cast her, to herself.

What if she could avoid all of them for a while?

She logged into her bank account and stared at the numbers for a while. They didn't change. Numbers didn't lie, though they didn't tell the whole story either. Sabrina hadn't spent that money on a whim. All her life she had been careful, until that chance came along…and vanished.

"Okay. What if I did something wild?"

There was no one to answer her. Sabrina felt silly, but strangely excited to say it out loud. She went to the website of Boxwood once again, checking for hotels. She assumed that around this time of year, every room in the picturesque village would be sold out, but she could always try one of the bigger towns close by.

Not finding anything that appealed to her, she checked for flights next.

There was one that left for Holbrooke, the closest bigger city, tomorrow. From there, it was another two-hour car ride.

Her fingers trembled as she hovered over the button.

This was crazy. She didn't have the time to indulge in a leisurely vacation or a trip down childhood memory lane.

But Sabrina wanted it so much. With her dreams and investments going up in flames, she needed a safe place, somewhere she could have at least one more lovely Christmas. It wasn't too much to ask for, was it? Speaking of safe places…An idea came to her.

Perhaps she could do something even crazier. Miracles could happen around this time of year.

·♥·♥·♥·♥·♥·

She didn't dream of the train that night. Sabrina barely slept at all after finishing her travel preparations and packing a couple of suitcases. She might still be deep in denial about her situation, but at least she was doing something. If this panned out…Sabrina didn't finish the thought for fear of jinxing the idea. People in her profession were superstitious for a reason.

Around four a.m., she got up to take a quick shower, get dressed and make herself a coffee she had with the delicious brownie. No regrets.

She'd have the rest of her life for them, should she find out she had made another major mistake.

The cab she had ordered online arrived on time. The driver didn't seem in the spirit at all, no decoration, no Christmas music. Sabrina didn't mind. She couldn't have been more excited.

She was really doing this, running away from the news that would break sometime soon, running back home. True, it wasn't her home anymore, not at this moment, but maybe there was a way she could still turn things around.

She had booked the earliest flight she could get, hoping she wouldn't run into too many people that recognized her.

"Hey, Sabrina!"

So much for that. She considered ignoring the man scrambling after her, but she really wanted another coffee before the flight. Perhaps he'd go away if she talked to him for a moment? Suppressing a yawn, she turned around.

"Is it true that Emily Davis is going to get the part in *The Stranger Next Door?* Man, that's not fair."

She easily recognized the tactic, him trying to get her to say something negative about Emily that could be construed into a feud.

"She works as hard as I do. I wish her all the best."

"Isn't it true that with your latest project falling through, you are in a bit of a bind financially?"

It was too early for this kind of question, and it was none of his business anyway.

"I'm good. Actually, I'm on the way to my vacation, so, if you don't mind..."

"Sure. Safe travels."

"Thanks."

13

She decided to go through security and have her latte on the other side.

·•·♥·♥·♥·

The closer Sabrina got to her destination, the more she was filled with a mix of excitement and the tiniest bit of apprehension. If she went through with her plan, would there be anything to do for her in town? It wasn't exactly an easy commute back to L.A. Did it mean she was giving up?

On the other hand, she couldn't continue like her latest failures didn't matter. If she managed to sell the condo and a few other assets, she would still be able to buy her childhood home back from the Connors. Their child was older now, and perhaps they wanted to move to a bigger city.

She wasn't above using her fame to persuade them, even given that she had to be careful with what was left of the fortune. And perhaps it was a good opportunity to find out if she'd miss L.A., more importantly, if L.A. was going to miss her.

It was dark when she left her destination airport to pick up her rental car. A few snowflakes were dancing in the wind. She breathed in the cold air. Her surroundings felt unreal, though the cold was not. Sabrina had brought the warmest clothes she owned, which had mostly stayed folded in a far corner of her closet as she didn't need them at home. Or what had been her home in the past years. She wasn't so sure anymore.

The change of scenery felt exciting and comforting, and she ignored the warning voice that told her it might be better to stay in a hotel room and continue the journey the next day.

Sabrina was eager to arrive in her old hometown, in a place where no one would judge her calorie intake, and it was unlikely anyone had even heard that she'd been in the running for the movie. It was dark, but not too late, and perhaps she could catch the Connors before dinner. Read the room, so to speak, return the next day with an offer.

The drive out to Boxwood led her through some construction and detours, not nearly as idyllic as she remembered.

The last part ran through a forested area, the road narrowing as it wound up to the higher situated neighborhoods in the hills. Any time, she would see the illuminated village...

To Sabrina's disappointment, there were nowhere near as many lights in the trees and the front of businesses as she remembered. To her childhood self, it had always looked magical. She drove farther, thinking that perhaps everything looked bigger and more magical to a child.

It would all be different once she came to Main Street where the Christmas market was located, and not far from it, the station where the magic train started its journey. No one ever got lost in Boxwood.

It only took her another fifteen minutes to arrive at the house she'd grown up in.

Sabrina parked on the other side of the street, watching in awe for several minutes. There it was, the cheer she'd found missing from other areas of town, or really, her life in the past few years. Either the Connors had more children now, or they really loved Christmas. So many lights, reindeers, candy canes—and a giant tree, lit up with hundreds of lights.

She realized that there was a parking lot where the neighbors' house had stood, and every spot was taken. A couple that had just arrived pulled their suitcases to the front door. Not the Connors. What did that mean? Did they have friends over for a party? She might not have picked the best moment.

Sabrina straightened. Or perhaps it was perfect. What if the festive mood helped her case? She had to make decisions soon, and the sooner she had clarity, the better. She had to act while she still had some of that fame to coast on.

15

She got out of the car and barely avoided slipping on a patch of ice. Sabrina looked around, and, grateful that no one had seen the almost accident, she walked towards the front door. It was decorated with a wreath and a welcome sign.

Sabrina rang the doorbell, only to realize that the door was open. Confused, she stepped inside. People trusted their neighbors in small towns, but this might be a little too much...? The entry didn't look familiar at all. She walked right up to the counter.

Wait...Since when is there a counter?

"Good evening! You have a reservation...oh."

Sabrina could always tell the exact moment when people recognized her. Of course, she'd lived here, so she had expected to find familiar faces. She didn't know the woman wearing a skirt and an ugly Christmas sweater that wasn't ugly at all.

If Sabrina hadn't been as impatient and tired as she was, she might have paid more attention to how the soft fabric hugged her figure. The green wool presented a nice contract to her auburn-colored hair that fell in waves to her shoulders. Warm brown eyes were wide with the obvious surprise.

Despite her exhaustion, Sabrina did notice.

Given her flustered reaction, the woman knew who Sabrina was. The soft blush to her cheeks might come from the fact that it was really warm in the place, not that Sabrina was complaining. Not about the temperature, anyway.

"I don't have a reservation. I was hoping I could talk to Mr. and Mrs. Connor?"

Realization dawned on the other woman's face.

"The Connors sold the house and moved away five years ago. I'm sorry, but I don't have a current address."

"Okay...Don't worry, that's fine." It wasn't, not at all, but she couldn't tell her. She'd have to regroup. Silence ensued as Sabrina was trying to come to terms with what she'd just learned.

"Who owns the place now?"

"That would be me. Excuse me, I'm being a terrible host. My name is Misty Duncan." She reached out a hand. "And you are Sabrina Russell." Usually, Sabrina felt a tad uncomfortable when someone spoke her name with this much awe, but she was tired and anxious enough to let it slide. At least, Misty Duncan was polite, and didn't ask her any questions—yet—about failed projects. She was cute, making Sabrina feel a bit more forgiving.

"Yes, I am," she confirmed. "This is a hotel now?" She'd been so single-mindedly focused on her mission she must have missed the sign—or it was covered in snow. That explained the multiple cars in the parking lot.

"A Bed & Breakfast," Misty explained. "We left things as close to the original house as possible. This home is one of the most beautiful ones in town, and I knew I had to have it when I first saw it. I walked right up to the owners, and fortunately for me, they were willing to sell."

So she didn't know that this was Sabrina's childhood home.

Since her first plan was out the window, Sabrina had to come up with a better one.

"Good for you," she said with what she hoped was a convincing smile. "Could I have a room?"

"Oh Gosh, I'm sorry again. We're all booked. I just gave away the last one, minutes before you arrived."

The couple she had seen earlier must have snatched it. Was it her destiny to always have the worst timing possible?

"That is...unfortunate." *Don't you know who I am*? wouldn't work here. Misty Duncan knew who she was, and she'd still made her point. "You don't happen to have a couch somewhere I could sleep on?"

For some reason, that made Misty even more flustered. Sabrina couldn't deny she enjoyed it, or at least, would have enjoyed it more under different circumstances. She needed a place to stay, and she needed to come up with an offer Misty couldn't refuse—which was a lot more difficult than negotiating with the Connors would have been. Misty had launched a business here, a successful one from the looks of it. Sabrina suppressed a sigh.

"I could ask around," Misty offered. "While you're waiting, how about a hot chocolate?"

"Thank you. I'll take you up on your offer, but no drink. I've been traveling all day. I need to get into a room as soon as possible."

"I understand. Have a seat over there," she pointed to a couple of armchairs next to another decorated tree. "I'll make some calls."

Sabrina thanked her again, walked over to the armchairs and sat down, suppressing a relieved sigh at the immediate comfort. She closed her eyes for a second, nearly dozing off in the warmth surrounding her. She took in the decorations on the tree, delicate spheres and stars made from glass, and...*wait a minute*. She got to her feet, determined to raise the subject, when Misty appeared in front of her. Sabrina could tell that she didn't have good news.

"I'm really sorry—again. I'm sounding like a broken record, right? There are no vacancies anywhere near."

A part of Sabrina wanted to argue and snipe, until Misty continued, "You could probably get something if you want to drive back all the way to the airport. In case you don't...I don't know, it's probably not what you're used to, but I have a guest room in my apartment upstairs. It wouldn't cost you anything, of course. I'll put another table in the breakfast room tomorrow, and only charge the breakfast?"

Sabrina was almost asleep on her feet, and those were far too many words. They included guest room, free, and breakfast, though, which sounded tempting.

"I don't know..." Then again, she didn't feel like driving back to the airport either. If she took Misty Duncan up on her offer, she could at least get a good night's sleep soon. "But I guess it will do for one night." Okay, perhaps it was a little snippy. Misty's face fell ever so slightly before her smile was back in place. "Now I'm the one who's sorry," Sabrina said with regret. "It's been a long day."

"Don't worry about it. Your luggage is in the car? I can have someone get it for you."

"I can do it myself. You think I could leave the car parked on the other side of the street?"

"Oh, that's perfect, but let me help you."

At this point, Sabrina was too tired to protest. Building a rapport with Misty would only help her cause, wouldn't it?

·♥·♥·♥·♥·♥·

Sabrina was beyond curious, but she was also aware that she had to be careful if she wanted her plan to work. That meant she'd better continue that conversation after a good night's sleep.

"Thank you for all your help," she said after they had brought her luggage inside. "I think I'm going to turn in early."

"Of course, you must be exhausted. I'll have your table ready tomorrow, and if you need anything, please let me know."

I need this place to be my home again, but we'll talk about that tomorrow.

She followed Misty upstairs to the guest room, which was actually a guest suite. Even as tired as she was, Sabrina couldn't help the pang of a bittersweet emotion when she realized it was her parents' old bedroom that Misty—or the Connors?—had converted into the suite. Down the hall had been her own bedroom, now apparently Misty's. Another staircase still led to the small attic.

"Is everything okay?" Misty asked quietly, too observant for Sabrina's taste.

"Yes, of course. Thanks again. I promise, I'll be out of your hair tomorrow."

"Don't worry about it. Just take your time."

Chapter Three

Just take your time? When Misty went to check the breakfast room to push two tables together and then carry another one inside, she replayed that conversation in her head. It was beyond surreal. Sabrina Russell was sleeping in her guest suite, under her roof.

It was only logical that Misty hadn't slept all night, and not just because she wanted the breakfast room to be ready for all her guests, like every day.

Like every resident, she knew that Sabrina had grown up in Boxwood but left it for Los Angeles many years ago. She'd stopped coming around after her parents died, and her childhood home was sold. Misty had fallen in love with the building the moment she saw it. Once she learned who it had belonged to, it seemed like a sign.

She resisted the urge to pinch herself. Even coming off a several-hour trip, Sabrina Russell was simply stunning. Misty was proud of herself for not losing her cool, even though it had been borderline for a moment. But Sabrina hadn't come here for admiration—in fact, she hadn't mentioned her reason for coming to Boxwood at all.

It was possible that she'd heard about the dire situation the town found itself in. Her celebrity status might be helpful to draw attention to the subject. Or perhaps she was taking a vacation in a familiar spot? Misty shook her head. She loved living here, running her own business, but Sabrina had left a long time ago. Perhaps she had some business to take care of, and none of it was any of Misty's business.

She jumped when the door opened, and her sister Lori walked inside.

"Good morning. I'm sorry I'm this early, but it started snowing again, and I thought I better get ahead of it."

"That's okay. You can go up to the kitchen. I'll be right there. Would you mind starting the coffee?"

Lori had joined Misty in the business right after her divorce, supporting her all the way. Back then, opening a Bed & Breakfast in a dwindling town seemed like a terrible idea, but they had worked hard and made it work. Boxwood's economy had been doing better than expected, until recently.

"Of course not. Are you redecorating?" Lori asked, taking in the new arrangement of tables.

"Not really. I'll be right up."

"All right." Lori left for Misty's private quarters.

The breakfast buffet would be open in about an hour and a half. Outside, there was barely a hint of dawn, so Misty assumed she'd have time to explain yesterday's surprise to Lori. She gave the room another cursory look and went upstairs as well.

In her kitchen, Lori had started the coffee and was setting the table. She poured a cup for her and Misty each, when after a knock on the door, Sabrina walked inside.

"Oh...I'm sorry, I didn't know you had a guest," she said at the same time coffee sloshed over the rim of Lori's cup.

"Oh, hey, just ignore me," Lori said, giving Misty a quizzical glance. "I'll clean this up."

"Ms. Russell, my sister Lori. Lori, this is—"

"Sabrina Russell. Don't be rude, Misty, you don't have to introduce her. Excuse me, please."

Misty blushed hotly while Lori reached for a paper towel to clean up the coffee from the floor. She washed her hands and then returned to the table.

"Okay, I'm sorry about that. I'm Lori Duncan. Welcome to *Misty's Maison Inn*."

"Nice to meet you." Sabrina shook her hand, cautious, as if she still didn't know what to make of the scene.

Misty cleared her throat, willing herself to remember that regardless how rich and famous...and gorgeous Sabrina Russell was, she was also a guest. Nothing more and nothing less. She would get over herself and treat her as such.

"Breakfast will be ready downstairs in an hour. I have your table ready. Is there anything else I can help you with?"

"An hour is long. Are you hungry? How about you sit down with us?" Lori suggested. "I swear I won't spill any more coffee, but I could make you an omelette."

Sabrina gave her a gracious smile. "Thank you. That's not necessary—the omelette, I mean," she continued after Misty barely suppressed a relieved sigh. "I'll have a coffee if that's okay."

"Of course, but I'm telling you, you're missing out."

"I don't want to impose, and I'm really not hungry."

"You're not, I promise you."

Someone's stomach was growling, and Sabrina gave a self-conscious laugh.

23

"I suppose that makes me a liar. I'm sorry, and...You're very kind. An omelette sounds perfect, actually."

"Don't worry, it's no problem." With a triumphant grin in Misty's direction, Lori got another set of dishes out of the cabinet. She served Sabrina coffee in a mug decorated with Santas before she started breaking eggs in a bowl.

Surreal didn't even begin to describe it.

"Thank you for having me," Sabrina said after taking a sip of her coffee. Her expression reflected pure bliss.

All of a sudden, Misty had trouble concentrating. Self-conscious, she focused on the empty plate in front of her.

"I really appreciate it. I wanted to get an early start. I understand you're booked, but I don't think the guest room is working for me. I'll try to find something closer to the airport later today."

Of course. She would do whatever it was she had come here to do and leave Boxwood as soon as she could. Misty couldn't say she was surprised. Disappointed, for sure, but not surprised.

"Is there anything I can do?" she asked anyway.

"I'm sorry, that came out wrong," Sabrina apologized. "The rooms are lovely. It's just that...There are a lot of memories here."

"Oh, I can imagine. Your room must be familiar, then." It was starting to get tiring, trying wordlessly to get Lori to be a tad more diplomatic.

"It is. I have to admit, I didn't expect to spend the night in my parents' old bedroom."

"I can see how that would be difficult," Lori acknowledged, "but it will be hard to find any rooms in the vicinity at this time of year."

Sabrina looked dejected. Perhaps this situation was as unreal to her as it was to the other two people in the room. Misty wondered once more what had brought her here, around Christmas of all times.

"It was a silly idea. I'd been thinking about the train, and I guess I felt nostalgic."

"You mean the Christmas train?" Misty asked. "Then your timing is perfect. This year will be the last time it runs."

In the time she'd spent here, she had soon learned that the annual ride was a cherished tradition. Residents would wait on the platform and cheer its arrival even if they didn't go on board, and local vendors were selling sweet and savory treats, eggnog, and mulled wine. She hadn't expected Sabrina's face to fall, given the fact that she hadn't been to Boxwood in years.

"The last time?" Sabrina echoed. "What happened?"

"They've been struggling to get the funding together, and while everyone loves it, they haven't been able to sell all the tickets in the past couple of years," Misty explained, irrationally wishing she could do something about Sabrina's disappointment. "It's really sad, this has been around for such a long time...but we'll still have the tree lighting, and the Christmas market."

"A lot of tourists now prefer the big resorts. We're lucky to still be fully booked this year, but that could change soon," Lori added. "Did you ever go on the train as a child?"

"Oh yes. Many times." Sabrina took a deep breath. "It's really all about money, isn't it?"

This time, Misty was searching her sister's gaze for help. Strange to think that a rich and famous Hollywood actress would worry so much about the end of a small-town tradition. Or was it? For most people, her and Lori included, Christmas traditions new and old were linked to many, sometimes mixed emotions. Misty assumed fame did not make a big difference.

"Sadly, it often is that way," Lori said. "But it doesn't have to be. Since you're already here, and the train will run one more time, why don't we make it the best Christmas ever?"

When she didn't get much of a reaction, she urged, "Come on, ladies. It's Christmas. Let's believe in a little magic?"

Misty couldn't say it out loud, but the fact that Sabrina Russell sat at her kitchen table, wearing that wistful smile, was almost more magic than she could handle. To her surprise, Sabrina answered first.

"I'd love to. Let me know if there's anything I can do to help."

So it was decided.

·♥·♥·♥·♥·♥·

"Miracles do happen at Christmas," Lori declared once Sabrina had left to explore the town on her own for a bit. "This is yours. Now go for it."

"Go for what? We have to serve breakfast," Misty mumbled, aware she was blushing.

"That's all you can say? Sabrina Russell shows up at your doorstep, spends the night in your guest suite, and you want to go to work?"

"She's a guest. And the business isn't going to run itself."

"You're forgetting that you have a capable partner, and employees. So, tell me, what's the plan? Are you going to ask her out?"

"Ask her out?" Misty realized that her voice had gone up a notch. "I don't know her."

"Then you better make use of the time. Look, I'm not suggesting you propose to her, but you've had a huge crush ever since you first saw her. This is a chance that will never come back."

Did Lori really think she needed to remind her? "There is no chance, and I'd be foolish to think otherwise," Misty said with all the conviction she could muster. "I'll help her best I can, and maybe she can do something for us. If she really wants to spend Christmas here, that could help the town."

Lori laughed. "It's good that someone has the town's best interests at heart."

"I do. Don't make fun of me for it."

"I never would," Lori said, now serious. "I wasn't kidding about the other subject either."

She was right. Neither Misty's feelings for Boxwood, their home, nor Sabrina Russell, the woman she had been enchanted with at first sight, were a laughing matter.

But she had to keep her priorities in mind—and still come to terms with the fact that Sabrina was really here.

Chapter Four

When she knocked on the door to Misty Duncan's kitchen, Sabrina had been determined raise the subject that had brought her here and ask her about her price. Make it quick, set up a contract the same day perhaps...

Now it didn't look like any of it was going to happen soon. The sisters seemed so comfortable here in the place she'd once called home, Sabrina was almost jealous. On the bright side, Misty and her sister didn't seem to know or care that Sabrina's star was falling, crashing, to be truthful. Her celebrity status didn't impress them that much either, though she had to be grateful for the delicious impromptu breakfast.

They would have offered it to any guest because they were nice people.

Now—what?

Lori Duncan had suggested going out with a bang, at least where the Christmas train ride was concerned. Sabrina still couldn't believe that she'd picked its last year to spend the holidays in Boxwood. She couldn't seem to get away from endings, without ever arriving anywhere.

It wasn't much of a consolation that there were problems everywhere, even in what had felt like the safest place in the world at some point in her life.

At least, the town still showed itself defiant in the face of budget cuts and an uncertain future, which was a whole lot more than Sabrina could say for herself.

She walked past the church and the Christmas market that was closed at this hour. The few people that passed her by didn't recognize her.

What had possessed her, she wondered?

Would it have been better to stay, and fight—but for what? Had she been banging her head against walls all along, with no chance of ever getting through? Sabrina came to the train station where a small poster advertised the Christmas ride.

Coming soon...Get on the magic train while Santa brings the presents!

She stood in front of it for several minutes, as the wind picked up. The only thing warm were the tears on her face.

Everything good had to end, and she didn't need to come here for the lesson. Her parents were gone, her home, her career, and now her last connection to a time of wonder and believing that dreams could come true.

It was all gone.

And now she might not even be able to go through with her plans. Sabrina had been determined, fantasizing about coming home...She was hesitating to bring up the sale with the Duncan sisters, for reasons that weren't entirely clear to her.

"Hey. You made it."

Misty Duncan's cheerful voice put an end to her dwelling, and she hastily wiped her face before turning around.

"Are you okay?"

She hadn't done a good enough job.

"You keep asking me that," Sabrina said, forcing a smile. "But thank you, I'm good. This just caught me by surprise. Still."

"It means a lot to many people around here. Lori and I went a couple of times with friends. It is beautiful."

"Yes. Nevertheless, at some point, we have to grow up, right?"

"That doesn't mean we have to lose all the magic," Misty objected. "My sister exaggerates a bit sometimes, but she's right about one thing. We can make it special this year. I hope you don't feel obligated to anything though. I don't even know what your plans are."

"I think I'll stay for a bit. If I can help with anything, let me know."

"In that case, would you have dinner with me tonight?" Misty stopped as if she couldn't believe she'd said that. Sabrina waited patiently, the turn of events chasing her sadness as she suppressed a smile.

"I mean, just so we can discuss...We always have a toy drive before the train ride. And there's the tree lighting. We could brainstorm other ideas."

She still used a lot of words, but today, Sabrina found it beyond charming. If only she could convince her to sell. She'd give it her best shot. Besides, an evening in Misty's company wouldn't hurt either.

There had to be options. They could both have a home in Boxwood, somehow.

"I'd love to," she said.

·♥·♥·♥·♥·♥·

"Excuse me."

31

Misty looked up to see the young couple that had checked in the night before, standing at the counter. He was leaning close, whispering.

"I told my wife it's impossible, but she won't believe me. We didn't see Sabrina Russell earlier, did we?"

Misty was taken aback, unsure what to do next. Whatever had led Sabrina to come here, she certainly would want to do it in private.

The woman gave a somewhat pained smile. "Please, don't embarrass me," she said.

"What's embarrassing about it? We're just asking. I'm sure she wants to hide away from the headlines for a bit. I don't blame her. You read about it, right?" he said to Misty. "The studio dropped her gay movie, and now some other actress got a big role that was supposed to be hers...no wonder she's having a more modest vacation."

"Don't you worry about me. I'm not broke yet." Sabrina's arrival caused the woman to look at her feet in shame, though her husband was unfazed.

"So it really is you! It's so great to meet you."

"Yes, thank you. Likewise," she said with a polite smile. "Misty, can I talk to you for a second?"

"Yes, of course. If you'll excuse us?" She didn't wait for an answer but opened the door behind the counter with a sign that said *Private*. "Come with me please." When she had closed the door behind themselves, she said, "Wow. This kind of thing happens everywhere you go?"

Sabrina shrugged. "No one recognized me earlier, or if they did, they didn't approach me."

"I'm sorry. Unless it had been the police and they had a warrant, I wouldn't have told him anyway."

"That's good to know." Sabrina chuckled at Misty's promise, or perhaps just the way she had phrased it. Either way it was a welcome and beautiful sound. "I hope that the police aren't after me on top of everything, but thank you. I appreciate it."

Silence ensued, stretching to a point of slightly awkward.

"What he said...Maybe I should explain," Sabrina started.

"No, you really don't have to. I'm sorry things didn't work out, but you don't have to explain anything to me."

"Okay. I won't keep you any longer. You're busy."

"No. I mean, yes, I am, but..." Misty took a deep breath. "I'll talk to you later, okay?"

"Of course. I look forward to it. Formal or casual?" Sabrina asked.

"Excuse me?"

"The restaurant."

"Oh." That was making it real. She was going out to dinner with Sabrina. "Boxwood formal, not L.A. formal."

"Got it. I'll let you go back to work."

She left, and Misty sank into the next chair. What was she getting herself into? Better yet, what had Lori gotten her into? No, it wasn't entirely fair to put the blame on Lori. It was true, Sabrina's work had carried her through some more difficult periods in her life. She admired her. But she didn't know her.

No matter how intriguing the real Sabrina was, and how curious she was about her, Misty had to remember that tonight wasn't a date.

She wanted to help Boxwood, and it seemed that Sabrina cared about her hometown. That was all there was—all there could be. Just because it was Christmas, it didn't mean she should get her hopes up, especially when the closing of the train tracks was already a done deal.

Once the Christmas train was gone, would she still have a full house around the holidays? Would they even be able to keep the inn?

Maybe Sabrina wouldn't be the only one having to make difficult decisions. Misty heard the bell of the front desk, and she pushed those unpleasant thoughts aside.

Chapter Five

S abrina wasn't exaggerating earlier this morning, when she said that if was difficult to be in this room—like now, getting ready for an evening out on the town. Perhaps she had hoped for too much, wanted too much.

She still wanted this house, if only to have a place where time stood still, when she hadn't faced so many disappointments. She was going to raise the question with Misty tonight.

The dress she'd put on wasn't this year's fashion, but she remembered Misty's comment regarding the restaurant being "Boxwood formal," thinking it would do. It had been a while since she'd done her own hair and make-up before going out to dinner, to a place where she knew no paparazzi would be waiting. The prospect had her excited despite all.

Misty was dressed up in a pretty dark blue dress, still behind the counter. She did something of a doubletake when Sabrina came down the stairs, even though she caught herself right away.

"There you are," she said, looking pensive as she held Sabrina's gaze, making her wonder if she had underestimated Boxwood's current restaurant scene. For Hollywood, her top and pants would certainly qualify as casual. But this wasn't Hollywood. She was going to have dinner with a friendly—and attractive—Boxwood resident. To brainstorm, Sabrina reminded herself. And to hopefully convince her to sell.

"Is this okay?" she asked anyway. "I can change."

"No, it's perfect." Misty cleared her throat. "I'll just have to wait for Lori, and we can go."

"I'm here!" Lori came all but jogging into the room, casting Sabrina an unabashed grin before she turned to her sister. "You two have a nice evening. I'm not going to wait up for you."

Misty looked like she barely kept herself from rolling her eyes before she got into her coat and picked up a scarf.

It was the moment Sabrina realized they were not going to take a car.

"How far are we going?" she asked.

"It's just down the street, don't worry. You'll be fine."

Sabrina looked down at her shoes, doubtful, but when Misty stepped out from behind the counter, she saw that she was wearing a pair of ankle boots too.

"It's not that cold tonight, and the sidewalks are all clear," she promised.

"All right then. Let's go."

The evening was indeed unusually mild for the season. They walked in companionable silence, each of them hanging on to their thoughts. Sabrina's were still pierced by a confusing mix of melancholy and excitement. With these emotions came the realization that she liked the new owner of her childhood home, which only made things more complicated. She had expected to negotiate with the Connors, make them an offer they couldn't refuse.

Misty hadn't promised too much, and about five minutes later, they walked through a gate and entered a courtyard. The sign above the restaurant said, *The Dining Car*. Sabrina halted so abruptly Misty almost collided with her.

"You remember this?"

She did.

"Of course. We always came at least once around the holidays. They used to have wonderful decorations." She laughed, remembering herself as a child staring in awe until her parents gently tugged on her hand and they'd follow the server to their table.

"They still do. You must stumble onto something familiar everywhere you go."

Misty sounded wistful. Sabrina couldn't help wondering what the reason was, or what kind of Christmas memories the town inspired in her.

"I do. Thank you, this was a nice idea. I came to Boxwood without much of a plan." It wasn't entirely true, except she hadn't given much thought to her dining choices.

"You're welcome. Now, let's see what's on the menu."

·♥·♥·♥·♥·♥·

Edie Madison, the owner of *The Dining Car*, greeted her with a bright smile.

"Misty, so nice to see you here. And...Sabrina, is that really you? It's been too long. Come here."

Sabrina let herself be embraced by the older woman. The quick sad visit when she finalized the sale with the Connors had been the last time that she'd seen Edie.

She didn't want to think about it now.

"I think Misty made a reservation."

Sabrina thought she'd noticed the tiniest of reaction when she called Misty by her first name. Edie didn't need to speculate. Sabrina needed to be by herself, reconsider her priorities. A date wasn't on the list, though a part of her wished that someday in the future she could have something real, with someone who cared about her more than they did about her fame. It was all bound to fade. She needed something permanent.

"Yes, of course. Follow me, please."

The table by the window was tastefully decorated with a small centerpiece including a candle and a couple of shiny Christmas ornaments. Looking outside, Sabrina remembered the view from the times she'd come with her parents.

There was a wood-burning fireplace, and the tree was always stunning. So many lights, delicate ornaments, the angel tree topper. It would have been easy to forget why she'd come here in the first place.

Maybe Sabrina wanted to forget, because bringing up the sale would only serve to shatter the cozy atmosphere. She hadn't run the numbers with the bank yet. Since the property housed a successful business, the price had likely gone up.

"I am sorry about earlier," Misty said. "They shouldn't be gossiping about you."

"It's not your fault. I don't know, perhaps it's not so bad that someone still wants to talk about me?" She could sense Misty's curiosity. "It's not as bad as it sounds in the media," Sabrina finally said, in need to convince herself—and Misty, if she wanted her to consider Sabrina as a prospective buyer. "A project fell through, and I didn't get that one job. Next year will be different."

"Still, before Christmas, that's rough. I got fired from my job before I came here."

"Oh…I'm sorry." Sabrina wasn't sure how far Misty wanted to go into the subject.

"It's okay, now. They were wrong. I thought about suing them, but then I put my savings into *Misty's Maison Inn* instead. I don't want to think about what could have been anymore. I'm happy here."

"Oh." Sabrina realized that she was repeating herself. "That's a good thing." Was it that easy? Feeling happy, at home. She couldn't remember when she'd last felt like that, especially around Christmas. "I was happy here," she admitted. "But that was a long time ago."

"You have an amazing career in L.A. Many friends, I'm sure."

Misty's cheeks had a subtle blush to them. Often, the admiration from people who didn't know her, who had barely taken a glimpse behind the shiny surface, bothered her. It was different with Misty who was so kind and gentle about it. That, Sabrina could handle.

Besides, Misty was a professional in her own right.

"I'd be wrong to complain. But tell me about the most amazing Christmas we're going to make happen. There's really no chance for the Christmas train to continue?"

"I'm afraid it doesn't look good. We have a full house this season, but it's not guaranteed for the future. Some remember your parents and how much they gave to the community. Many want to see the train for the last time. Once that goes away..." Misty shrugged.

A waitress came by with a bottle of wine, the label familiar to Sabrina. It wasn't cheap to say the least.

"I didn't order this," Misty said, sounding confused. She corrected herself quickly. "I didn't mean that my guest isn't worth it, but I didn't..."

"It's on the house," the waitress, a woman of about twenty-five, said cheerily. "It's not often that we have a celebrity in the house, let alone one who was born and raised here."

"Tell Edie, thanks, but we'll be okay." Sabrina felt her face heat. Boxwood was the last place where she wanted to be handed things for her name. Sure, she'd thought about using it to her advantage but not here, not after what Misty had just told her about the local businesses.

Edie Madison joined them at their table again, quickly dissolving any awkwardness.

"She heard you," Edie said, "and please, let me do this for you. We love having a Russell here again. We missed you." She laughed. "No offense, Misty. You know we love you too, right?"

"It's fine. Thanks, Edie," Misty said, amused.

"Good. Now, it's Christmas time, please accept a gift, and enjoy."

"Thank you."

The waitress poured the wine for them, and she and Edie left.

Misty raised her glass. "All right then, to the best Christmas ever!"

Sabrina clinked her glass against Misty's before she sat it down again. "I'm all for that, but we were interrupted. My question is, how can I help?"

For a few seconds, Misty simply held her gaze. Maybe she wasn't sure what to say.

"I hate to be so blunt, but money would help. Okay, now that's out of the way, I was wondering...You grew up here, people love you. I think your presence would do a whole lot of good."

"My presence...On the train?"

"Perhaps. There's also the tree lighting, a Christmas concert, a play, and the toy drive." Misty winced and took a sip of her wine. "I crossed a lot of boundaries in a couple of sentences. I can see that in your face."

"That's fine," Sabrina assured her. "It's just that...it's been a while that I've been taking part in those. I actually was in the play for a few years. If it helps, of course, I'll join you." She wasn't sure how it would go, given her long absence from Boxwood and its traditions, but Sabrina was willing to give it a try. She needed to feel useful. If her contribution helped the town, even better.

Misty looked relieved and thoughtful at the same time. Maybe now, when they were both mellowed by wine and the spirit of the season, would be a good time to raise the question of a sale.

To Sabrina's relief, the waitress returned with their plates. No, not tonight. It was too early to talk about drastic changes. Misty said she was happy here. It didn't sound like she needed a change as badly as Sabrina did. She needed a convincing offer, something they'd both benefit from.

"That would be amazing, but please, don't think we want to exploit your celebrity status. Whatever you're comfortable with."

"I appreciate that. Thank you. Did you have something specific in mind?"

"To be honest, no, not yet. Would you mind saying a few words at the tree lighting? Or coming with us on that last train ride? How would you feel about us putting your name on a few flyers? A photo, maybe? I'm sorry, here I go again, crossing boundaries."

"No, don't worry." Sabrina couldn't help smiling. At least some people still wanted to be associated with her. She was grateful for Misty allowing her to connect to her home again. She was happy to spend time with her, period. "It's no problem. Can I ask you a personal question?" Talk about crossing boundaries, but Sabrina was curious.

Misty sat up a bit straighter, though she nodded. "Sure. Ask away."

"You started the B&B with your sister a few years ago."

"That's right."

"Is there...anyone special in your life?" The answer to that question could potentially be relevant to Sabrina's plans. A significant other might make a difference as to how Misty looked at the offer Sabrina was eventually going to make. *Right. That's the only reason to ask.*

"There was," Misty responded. "They thought I should try to get back into the job market rather than waste my last savings on a dream."

"I'm sorry."

"Don't be. It was for the better. I'm here, I have my business. Besides, I got to meet you, and we're getting a free bottle of wine, so all is good."

Sabrina detected a hint of melancholy. Misty had made herself at home in Boxwood after a disappointing detour. The situation wasn't the same for Sabrina. Nothing would bring back her parents. She had a choice to honor their memory. She cast a look outside the window, where it had started to snow. The mountains gleamed white in the distance.

"Okay. As for the events you mentioned, I'm in. Maybe we have a chance to raise some money for the train as well? Just one caveat—I will draw the line at a kissing booth."

"Now that's a shame." The self-conscious expression on Misty's face a second after she'd uttered the words spoke volumes. "I didn't mean...Wow, I shouldn't drink while discussing business."

"Don't worry, I got you. And it's not just business...I'd like to think of it as making friends."

Misty gave her a grateful smile. "Friends. Of course." She hesitated a few heartbeats before she continued. "Since I answered your question...friend...is there anyone special in your life? Because I'm pretty sure the tabloids can't be trusted at all."

"You'd be right about that," Sabrina said, amused. "The truth is so much more boring than you imagine. I love my job. I work a lot, or at least I used to until recently. There's no time to do everything the magazines allege I do."

"I imagine. Your work means a lot to many people, including me."

"Yeah." Sabrina suppressed a sigh. "I wish I could have done more."

"Don't give up," Misty said. "You do have more power than most people. You can change things to the better."

Was that the truth, or just the starry-eyed view of a younger woman on a cold reality?

"The project that fell through...people told me how important they thought it was, and when it was time to act, they thought it was too controversial. Then it wasn't controversial at all, and the only problem was my age."

"That is so ridiculous—on their part, of course. It's their loss. There will be another project for you...or other investors."

"Like there will be for the Christmas train?" Sabrina winced, her own tone sounding too sharp and judgmental to her ears. "I'm really sorry."

"Don't be. None of this is your fault."

No, but perhaps she didn't like to face the idea that she'd run from all responsibilities when there were still options.

No. Emily getting the role was the signal that The Powers That Be had given her. Sit down, be silent, accept your fate.

"You're not wrong. I'm tired. A lot of people who promised to have my back, didn't."

"Well, that changes right now. It's Christmas, and you have me. We'll create something special. I promise you."

It sounded so good. Sabrina needed good in her life, so she was willing to believe it, even though she feared it might all end the moment she told Misty the truth.

Not yet.

She enjoyed her company too much.

Chapter Six

Misty could still remember the first time she saw Sabrina Russell on the big screen, Sabrina's big break when she played a young ice skater at the beginning of a brilliant career. She had appeared in a few TV shows before, in one of them as the teenage daughter in a family sitcom. Finally, she starred in *Dreams of Gold*, the movie that would not only change her life, but also Misty's. She had fallen hard for her, even though the obligatory male love interest came with every one of Sabrina's roles. Misty didn't care, because she had enough fantasy and appreciation, spell-bound by Sabrina's talent.

It was an exciting time as she'd started to explore her own identity, her crush both thrilling and safe. It was even more meaningful to her after Sabrina's own coming-out.

Since then, Sabrina had used whatever influence she had to bring more women directors, writers, and producers to the table.

The power structures in her chosen field put a limit to her efforts, especially when she tried to put together the funds for a blockbuster movie led by two women in a romantic relationship. Not only were the protagonists attracted to each other, Sabrina had the audacity to make them forty-something.

Sabrina was still trying to do the right thing.

Misty still admired her for many reasons.

Tonight, Sabrina had asked her if she had someone special in her life. Of course she'd only been making conversation, but Misty's mind was still reeling.

She had thought she could sneak past the living room where Lori was waiting up for her, but no such luck.

"Hey. How did it go?"

Lori laid her paperback, a romance novel from one of her favorite authors, aside.

"Pretty well," Misty replied. "Sabrina agreed to come to the toy drive, the tree lighting, and other suggestions I made. She only drew the line at a kissing booth." Misty relayed parts of the conversation to her sister.

"You really told her it's a shame she doesn't want to raise money getting kissed by strangers?" Lori laughed. "That's...a bit obvious."

Misty couldn't deny it.

"You're incorrigible."

"Yeah, I know. How about a nightcap? I want to hear more."

Still much too wired to sleep after her night out with Sabrina Russell, Misty accepted.

"Like I said, she'll join us for some of the activities, which will really help. If she's there, many others will come, and you didn't promise too much when you said we'll do something great this year."

"We could use great," Lori agreed as she got two glasses and a bottle of cream liqueur out of the cabinet. "I heard Donovan is coming to town soon."

"Donovan? Where did you hear that, and what does he want?"

Their investor and mostly silent business partner didn't interfere with the way they ran things. In fact, they had barely seen him since sealing the deal.

"I don't know, probably see how things are going around here, I assume. Betsy sent me an email, but she didn't know details. He's been making plans for the end of next week."

Misty leaned back against the couch. Lori was friends with Donovan's assistant. Betsy casually mentioning the impending visit might not mean anything—or it meant that Betsy felt the need to warn them.

"I'm not sure I want to think of the possibilities, but we can show him that business is good for now. With Sabrina's help, it will be even better. I've been transparent with her, about what we hope to achieve, and what role she could play in that. Pardon the pun."

"Hm."

"What does that mean?"

"You've been transparent with her about the other thing?"

"Oh, come on. That's Sabrina Russell we're talking about. She'd never be interested in me." Yet, she had asked that question. To make conversation, Misty reminded herself.

"What are you talking about? You are smart, successfully running your own business, and you're the kindest person I know. Even after Abby left you and your old company let you down, you still try to see the best in people. This might be exactly what Sabrina has been missing."

"That's all...speculation." It was dangerous to think otherwise. For their plans, and Misty's heart. "Even if she's missing anything, she's not looking to find it with me."

"That's why you spent all that time at *The Dining Car*, having a fancy dinner. I see."

"It's more complicated than that." Misty sighed. "I don't want to drive her away with my silly issues. It's such a miracle that she came to Boxwood this year."

"Caring for someone isn't silly. Why would that drive her away? Maybe you could give her another reason to stay."

"Stop it, will you?"

Lori shrugged, but Misty assumed she wasn't going to give up on the subject anytime soon.

If only there was the sliver of a chance...

"She is every bit as amazing as I imagined," she admitted.

"Now we're getting somewhere. I happen to know you imagined what she was like a lot. That movie of hers, *Dreams of Gold*? You watched it so many times you wore out the VHS tape."

"Come on, it wasn't that bad," Misty protested, though her teenage self would have no room to argue. Sabrina had played a young ice skater with Olympic dreams. Sixteen-year-old Misty had had an awakening.

Yes, they were adults now, but their lives still differed drastically. Sabrina would stay over the holidays and go back to her life. Misty had no use for heartbreak, especially from someone who had meant so much to her for a long time. Even if the thought was...more than tempting.

"Oh, it was."

"I was interested in ice skating," she tried. Lori wasn't buying it.

"Right. And you never made it to the ice rink until much later, but I bet you can still recite the movie."

"This conversation is over," she declared. "I'm going to bed. Don't forget that we have a lot of work in the coming weeks."

"You and Sabrina, you mean."

Misty shook her head. "I'm going to call the mayor tomorrow. Good night."

She heard Lori giggle as she left the room.

It was late, and she hadn't lied about the work to come, but what if she watched a few minutes of *Dreams of Gold*? Or *Dangerous Tide*, the suspense movie Sabrina had starred in afterwards? No, that would be too weird, Misty decided. She had to focus on the present, and Christmas, whatever it would bring.

·♥·♥·♥·♥·♥·

Back in LA, Sabrina would write a check rather than participate in activities like the ones she agreed to. She knew that her ability to do so, at least until now, mattered, too. The idea of helping the town raise money felt both exciting and heavy. It seemed like she couldn't run from responsibility after all, and this time, nothing could go wrong.

Nevertheless, she fell into a deep and dreamless sleep that night, smiling as she remembered the warm atmosphere at *The Dining Car*, Edie's welcome, and the pleasure of Misty's company.

She had said yes to everything quickly, too quickly maybe, but it felt right. She felt at home here, still, and at ease with her decisions, and the people around here. Perhaps, one of them more than others.

It wasn't like Sabrina was chasing admiration. In fact, she had run from the complicated emotions that her profession had caused her recently.

And in L.A., she would have never had dinner with a fan, which Misty obviously was. But they had a connection beyond that, their love for the town and its traditions, and Christmas.

Misty wanted it to be the best Christmas ever, but what if they could go beyond that?

Getting ready to go to breakfast, Sabrina smiled to herself. As if she hadn't gotten a dire reality check, her ambitions already went above the toy drive and tree lighting.

If they could raise enough money...What if the train didn't have to stop running?

Sabrina walked down the stairs, intent on finding the table Misty had reserved for her, but then changed her mind and knocked on the door of the sisters' private quarters.

A few seconds later, Lori opened, a smile spreading on her face.

"Sabrina, good morning. Come on in. We're having pancakes this morning."

"That sounds amazing." She didn't even try to deny that she'd been hoping for another invitation. "And please, if I keep taking advantage of your hospitality, I'd like to pay for breakfast."

"Nonsense." Lori made a dismissive gesture. "I throw something together every morning for Misty and me, and all I have to do is make a bit more. Given what you've said yes to, you're helping us so much more than we could ever pay back with pancakes and some bacon."

Sabrina couldn't keep the smile off her face as she walked over the threshold once more, eager for yet another treat—without counting calories—and just as eager, if not more, to see Misty again.

"In that case, I accept. Thank you so much."

For a long time, even before two of the biggest projects in her career fell through, Sabrina had felt like she was failing, herself, other women in her situation. By not maintaining her success like she should have, by not making it big enough, by not representing enough.

Here at home, it seemed like she had the perfect opportunity to start over. Maybe she'd finally forgive herself, realize that she had tried everything she could. And maybe helping the small town where she had experienced a safe and happy childhood, would turn things around, for her and the residents of Boxwood? Sabrina had more hope than she'd had in months.

And she had a partner who wouldn't let her down.

Funny how, within the span of a few days, Misty Duncan had become many things to her. Friend. Partner.

Sabrina appreciated her honesty. She had made no secret of the fact that having a famous person in their corner would help. Just like that, she had admitted it, and they moved on and spent a pleasant evening together...It was easy. Nothing much had been easy in recent months. For a little while longer, she'd ignore that it didn't work both ways, that she had yet to be equally honest. But not so soon—first she had a few events to attend. Sabrina hoped that her support would make the conversation she needed to have with Misty easier on both of them.

Once again, she sat down in the cozy kitchen while Lori poured some coffee.

"Did you sleep well?" she asked.

"Oh yes," Sabrina confirmed which seemed to please her host. She turned to the window as Lori prepared their breakfast. The sky was overcast outside, and it was snowing again. Perfect for all the winter activities around here.

"I had the chance to talk to Mayor Gaines for a few minutes...There you are." Misty had come inside, stopping at the sight of Sabrina.

"I invited myself to breakfast—again. I hope that's okay with you."

"Oh. Of course. I'm glad you're here."

Sabrina admired Misty's outfit, a skirt with boots, and a sweater that signaled Christmas, though a bit more muted than the one she had worn when Sabrina arrived. This one was dark blue with a star on it.

"So, you said you talked to the mayor?"

Sabrina had never met Alicia Gaines. The woman was in her fifties, she knew, and had replaced the previous mayor when he retired.

"I did. She's very excited that you're on board with our Christmas activities, especially the tree lighting. But you'll meet her before. If you are up for it…" Misty hesitated for a few seconds. "Would you join me at the Christmas committee later? I could introduce you to everyone, and we could get started…"

"Yes! Yes, I'd love that."

Her parents had taken her when she was a child, but eventually schoolwork and then, her career, took over. Sabrina loved Christmas, and everything it encompassed in Boxwood—that, and apparently, she had a hard time saying no to Misty.

"Imagine our surprise when we moved here and got the invitation," Lori said. "We are all in now, but at first it felt like we had stepped into a Christmas movie. There you go," she added and put plates with stacks of pancakes in front of Misty and Sabrina. "Chocolate with a hint of orange. I got the recipe from a romance novel."

Sabrina was amused, Misty, as it seemed, more flustered with Lori's not so subtle hints.

"She reads a lot of romance novels."

"And I'm proud of it," Lori returned. "Life is complicated enough. There's nothing wrong with a little escape."

Sabrina agreed, technically. Providing much needed escape was a part of her job. As to what Lori was saying between the lines…It was more complicated than that. Under different circumstances, Sabrina might have thrown all caution in the wind, but both she and Misty had so much at stake already.

She had to get it right this time. Which, for now, meant joining the Christmas committee and keeping other ideas in check. She held Misty's gaze, ridiculously content to see her blush. Even though she couldn't let herself get distracted, it was good to know that Sabrina Russell hadn't lost her touch.

"Thank you, Lori. These are delicious. And I'm a fan of romance myself."

Chapter Seven

She had to be dreaming, Misty thought when she introduced Sabrina to the members of the Christmas committee, some of which were already familiar to her as they had served on the committee for a long time.

The younger members were equally as excited to have Sabrina on board.

She was happy to sit and watch Sabrina interact with everyone, so at ease it felt like she'd always been a part of it. Like this was something she was meant to do, be here with Misty...She nearly shook her head at her silly musings. If she wasn't careful, she would start to believe Lori, and from there she could easily spiral into fantasizing about another dinner, a real date, that might end with a...kiss. Sabrina insinuating that she had understood those little hints between the lines didn't help. *And I'm a fan of romance myself.*

"Misty Duncan! Look what you've done. You are single-handedly saving Boxwood."

She flinched when Mayor Gaines, who had joined the meeting spontaneously, patted her shoulder.

"I didn't realize Boxwood needed saving. We're just trying to prepare for possible changes ahead, right?"

"Yeah. Mostly. But having Ms. Russell here matters a lot, and you made that happen. We are grateful for that, Misty."

Gaines' more sober tone was telling. Suppressing a sigh, Misty sat her cup down, the caffeine now giving her a rush of anxiety.

"Boxwood is Lori's and my home," she said. "Anything we can do to help. You really think things could change that fast?"

Her expression spoke volumes. "I hope they won't, Misty."

Sabrina, who had probably overheard a part of their conversation, came over to them.

"Mayor Gaines, it's so nice to meet you." After they shook hands, she continued. "I've heard about the train. Look, I'm willing to help with all the other activities, but what if we could use some of them to also raise more funds to keep it running?"

Alicia Gaines looked doubtful.

"Our toy drive is aimed at helping our women's shelter, and low-income families in Boxwood, so there's no way we can take away from that."

"Of course not. I understand. What about the tree lighting? We could set up a booth, have a contest to raise money..."

"I've had many conversations with the representative of the company. I wish I could tell you something different, but they don't think it will be sustainable in the future and that it's better to rip off the Band-Aid, so to speak."

Misty could tell from Sabrina's expression that she wasn't willing to give up so soon, the realization warming her heart.

"But I'm open to ideas," the mayor concluded. "And yes, there could be a booth. I'll call the representative again. Now

I'm afraid I have to run, but please rest assured I appreciate everything you're doing."

Misty picked up her cup again, all thoughts of the near impossible task ahead fleeting when Sabrina smiled at her.

Not all hope was lost.

·♥·♥·♥·♥·♥·

The next few days were filled with a lot more activities than Sabrina had imagined when she booked her flight on a whim. She couldn't be more excited for Christmas, every place Misty took her to, a gift. They watched a rehearsal for the town's Christmas play where Sabrina signed autographs and took pictures with happy children and adults.

She had a quick session with a local photographer for the flyer announcing Sabrina's presence at the tree lighting, and Misty still managed to do a stellar job running the inn.

She seemed to have an endless well of energy, and Sabrina admired her for it as she sat in the inn's lobby with a coffee, watching her talk to some guests at the counter.

Truth be told, hanging around to wait for her in the evening had become another habit. She loved spending time with her.

Sabrina wasn't yet ready to draw conclusions from that—and besides, she was home for Christmas. What more reason did anyone need to be happy?

Misty had been busy all day, but she stepped out from behind the counter and came over to her.

Sabrina gestured for her to sit, and with a smile, Misty did.

"It's been quite a few days."

"True. And we're so grateful for everything you've done. Even if we can't bring back the train next year…"

"And that's still an 'if,'" Sabrina reminded her though they both knew the chances were slim.

"Yes. What I meant to say is it was all worth it. And since the days will only get busier, I think we deserve a break. I haven't made it to the ice rink yet this year, and I thought you might like to go?"

Sabrina was on her feet the next moment. She hadn't even imagined that would be a possibility during her stay.

"We could go now? I didn't bring skates, but I'm sure they still rent them out?"

"They do." She could only describe Misty's smile as joyful.

"So, you and Lori skate?"

"A little. Not like you, but I can manage to stay upright."

"I might be a bit rusty," Sabrina admitted, "so it's all good." How was it possible that Misty seemed to know exactly what she needed?

·♥·♥·♥·♥·♥·

It was already dark when they arrived at the ice rink, but a few skaters were still on the ice, others stood around the rink to watch, some with a hot beverage.

Sabrina couldn't lose sight of her plan, but this trip down memory lane wouldn't harm.

"I imagine you've seen *Dreams of Gold*, then," she teased Misty who gave her a self-conscious smile in return.

"A few times, yes."

It had been a while since Sabrina last had the opportunity to skate, but the basics still came back to her easily. It was glorious, reminding her of the confidence and optimism she had possessed in her younger years.

And she liked the company a lot better, though she realized Misty must have oversold her skating skills.

"This is still harder than it looks," she confessed.

Sabrina did a pirouette before she reached out a hand to her.

"It's not that hard. You don't have to do figures. Come here."

Reluctantly, Misty let go of the board, and they did a few steps together.

"You said you skate a little," Sabrina remarked, amused as she held on to her. "How much is a little?"

"Like I really wanted to learn when I saw you in that movie, and I gave it a few tries, but never got that far? I'm sorry. You're doing so much for us, and I thought this could be fun."

Misty sounded so miserable Sabrina wanted to hug her close. Because she was adorable at the same time. Because Sabrina wanted to be even closer to her, though that could be risky.

"It is. I love it. And don't worry, you're safe with me."

"Thank you."

Misty dared a few tentative steps. "You are so good at this. You must have practiced a lot."

"Not in many years, but I became pretty good when I had to practice for the role." Sabrina laughed ruefully, remembering how for some time, every waking moment was dedicated to making the character work. "I'll tell you a secret if you swear to keep it."

"You're safe with me too," Misty promised, clutching her arm tightly.

"Okay." Sabrina leaned closer, and Misty nearly stumbled. When she was steady again, Sabrina whispered to her, "I lied in my audition."

"What?!"

A couple skating past them gave them curious looks. Fortunately, they were so young they didn't recognize Sabrina right away. She shrugged.

"I actually did skate 'a little' but it wasn't nearly enough for what they wanted—but I wanted the part so much, so I hired a trainer."

"Wow."

"I was young and stubborn. In fact, it was kind of a *Dirty Dancing* situation."

"You had a crush on the trainer?" Misty asked, sounding intrigued.

"Yes, at first, but she was very...strict, and not at all interested in me. The only part that did work out was that she drilled some major skills into me in a short time, and I managed not to mess up."

"You were amazing." This time, Misty's tone had an almost dreamlike quality.

It was no secret that this movie had meant a lot to both of them. Even years after, Sabrina had received a lot of feedback from fans who had seen a metaphor in her character's overcoming of obstacles.

"I did all right," she acknowledged. "But that was a long time ago." And she would try her best not to but messing up was still a possibility.

"Some bad luck is not the end of everything, is it?"

"No. But I am rethinking my priorities...First of all, Christmas, right?"

"Yes."

Sabrina had the sudden urge to ask what Misty and Lori were doing on Christmas Day, but that moment, Misty slipped, and Sabrina had to step in and keep her from falling.

"It's all right. I got you."

She'd gotten her wish—they were standing so close she could see Misty's eyes widen, and her breath was warm on Sabrina's cheek. If she leaned in just a couple of inches...Sabrina wanted to, because Misty felt like home. Her lips looked soft and inviting, the smile chasing the deer-in-the-headlights expression beyond adorable, and damn it, she wanted to take risks...

"Hi! Misty, I didn't know you skated."

They stepped apart when Edie's daughter Jackie, who was also part of the Christmas Committee, greeted them. She had introduced them to the photographer who had taken Sabrina's picture for the flyer.

Sabrina had seen the hint of regret in Misty's expression, mirroring her own.

It might be risky. It might be worth it. She knew one thing for sure: She couldn't wait much longer to come clean, and not just because she still hoped to make the house her home again.

Chapter Eight

Had they really almost kissed? Misty couldn't help it, regardless of what lay ahead, she felt giddy with the realization. Sabrina, her celebrity crush turned friend-with-potential...maybe?

It was hard to imagine a reality where Sabrina wouldn't return to L.A. after the holidays to pick up her career again, but perhaps the welcome she had received here would make her want to visit more often?

Perhaps she would visit Misty again?

As they walked back home together past front lawns and windows decorated for the season, Misty couldn't be happier. The past few months had been marked by hard work and uncertainties, but her life had taken such a magical turn she found it easy to believe in a good outcome for all of them.

She wasn't so worried about the arrival of their investor anymore. They were having the best holidays ever, in no small part thanks to Sabrina's inspiring presence. He had to see that Boxwood, specifically the inn, was still worth his time and money.

"What are you thinking?" Sabrina asked, and she wondered how much she really wanted to hear.

"Many things. About how much has already changed since you arrived. The people here see that you care, and they are grateful. I know I am."

"Mostly, I'm sitting around and eating for free at your place," Sabrina joked.

"That's not true...I mean, it's true we don't want you to pay for breakfast, but you can't imagine how different it is to be on the committee now. Everyone feels, I don't know, lighter. Like, even if it's the last time for the train, we're not doomed. You did that. And everyone is looking forward to Christmas even more."

Misty knew she was, and she was wondering if she'd be crossing a line by inviting Sabrina. She and Lori always had dinner together on Christmas Eve, the day they exchanged gifts.

Christmas Day was dedicated to the guests who stayed at the inn. Sabrina was a guest all right, but she couldn't deny it would mean so much more.

"I don't think I did that much, but I'm happy to hear it." She shivered. "Wow, it got cold in just a few hours. I'm not used anymore to how quickly that happens here."

That, and most of her wardrobe seemed to be suitable for winters milder than they had in Boxwood.

"Would you like to come in for a hot chocolate?" she asked. "And perhaps I should take you shopping for a warmer coat."

Sabrina laughed. She sounded happy. "Both are good ideas, but let's start with the hot chocolate."

Misty wasn't sure if she should be disappointed or relieved when she saw Lori sitting in the kitchen, but at least she offered some more of that cream liqueur to go with the hot chocolate—and comments.

"I heard you engaged in Misty's favorite sport." Lori took a pot out of the cabinet to heat some milk. "How did that go?"

"It was perfect," Sabrina replied. "Misty has lots of potential."

"I bet."

Shaking her head, Misty admitted silently that she enjoyed the banter despite herself, and perhaps all other questions would have to wait until they had a clearer idea of the future, for the inn and Boxwood.

But there was still time until Christmas, and what if her wish could come true?

·♥·♥·♥·♥·♥·

Sabrina had excused herself after they'd shared the hot chocolate.

"I imagine that went well. Look at you, getting it all done and going on romantic dates with your favorite celebrity."

"Oh, come on. It wasn't a date. I just wanted to show my appreciation. Sabrina dropped everything to help us with this."

"Yes, and we appreciate it. On the other hand, it didn't look like she had much of a plan when she came here, so she probably enjoys having something to do," Lori pointed out. "So…"

It was only a matter of time before she was going to start fidgeting under her sister's inquisitive gaze. Misty decided she wasn't ready to share the sweet moment, and what had almost happened.

Would she have another chance? She could feel the heat rush to her face when her mind wandered back, Sabrina's gaze on her calm and serene, her beautiful eyes…No, she wasn't going to fool Lori, or anyone, much longer.

"I'm really tired," she said. "I'm going to bed too. We still have a lot of work to do until Christmas."

"That's your excuse for everything! Unfortunately, it's also the truth," Lori acknowledged with a sigh. "But it will be so worth it. Good night, Misty. Sweet dreams."

She winked, Misty rolled her eyes, and Lori burst out laughing.

But Misty made it out without having to reveal that reality was shaping up to be even sweeter than her dreams.

Or was it?

Long workdays, extra curriculum activities, and the excitement of having Sabrina under her roof, did the trick, and she fell asleep quickly. To no surprise, her subconscious brought her right back, and this time, there was no interruption. She could feel Sabrina's lips on hers, soft and warm against the chill of the night. The kiss started out gentle, as if she was asking for permission.

Misty pulled her closer to signal that she was all in, had been before they even met, because she wasn't fooling herself. Sabrina really was that kind, generous and inside-out gorgeous person she knew her to be. And every moment with her was confirmation.

The scenery switched from the ice rink to Misty's bedroom, and all of a sudden, she could no longer feel the cold, the kiss heated and passionate, making her knees weak. How could she not want more? Of course, she did. Fingers brushing over fabric, taking more liberties...Sabrina slid her hands into Misty's hair, and she gasped from the sheer pleasure of the gentle but firm touch, and what was to come...

She woke with a start, her heart racing. Really? Her subconscious had to end it there? Misty slumped back into her pillow, much aware of the disappointment. On the other hand, she would have to face Sabrina the next morning. If her dream had gone any further, it would have likely been awkward.

Nevertheless, she fell asleep again with a smile because it was so easy to imagine Sabrina in her arms.

·♥·♥·♥·♥·♥·

It had snowed more overnight. Distantly she'd heard the sound of a shovel against concrete. Sabrina had fallen back asleep, comforted by the thought that soon, this would be her home. This house. Boxwood. And Misty Duncan who had become an important part of the vision.

She could always go back and do another movie or TV show, maybe shoot in New York which was much closer. Toronto even.

To her disappointment, Misty wasn't present at breakfast this morning, but Lori had the table ready and poured a cup of coffee for them both.

"Don't get me wrong, it's beautiful here," she chatted. "But you must miss the sun and the warmth."

"Well, it can get nice and sunny here. And I've always liked seasons. There are so many great things about L.A.," Sabrina reminisced. "Boxwood is...different. Some things have changed, buildings and streets, but not that much. Everything still feels familiar."

"That must be great. Misty and I didn't lay down roots like that. We moved a lot when we were kids."

That was news to her. Sabrina wondered if that might make them more determined to hold on to the inn—and what it would mean for her and Misty in the long run. She had to make a move at some point. She also didn't want to destroy whatever, beautiful and likely fragile, was happening between them.

"That must have been exciting."

"And frightening. But we made new friends wherever we went, and our parents were always determined to make Christmas special. Our house was always open if someone needed a word, a hug, or a warm meal."

"That sounds great."

"It was. One time they invited a friend of ours with her two siblings and their parents, after the dad had lost his job. They were great. It's been almost ten years, but I still miss them every day."

"I understand."

"Yes, I know you do," Lori acknowledged. "Misty and I have tried out best to follow their example. You can't hold on to the past, but you can always make new traditions, right?"

Sabrina didn't say it out loud: She was going to try to do both. She hoped Misty and Lori would understand that she was doing it all with the best of intentions.

"I've got to run now. I'll see you at the tree lighting tonight."

"Yes, you will," Sabrina confirmed. "Have a nice day."

Lori got up, mug in hand.

"Just leave it," she said, making a sweeping gesture over the table. "I'll take care of it later."

"Thanks."

Sabrina sat a few minutes by herself as she finished her breakfast. She got up as well and stepped to the window.

Down on the street, Misty was clearing the sidewalk. Every once in a while, someone would stop by and talk to her. A man about her age stayed a little longer and said something that made her bend down and form a snowball she then threw at him. Both of them cracked up with laughter.

Feeling like an intruder, Sabrina stepped back, turning to the breakfast table before she started to clear the dishes away. She needed to do a bit more than just offer her name and face to raise funds. Besides, she didn't have that many plans until the evening.

·❤·❤·❤·❤·❤·

Since no one requested her presence this morning, Sabrina wandered into town again to take care of a few errands—as Christmas was fast approaching, she needed a few gifts for her generous hosts. She stopped to watch the preparations for the upcoming tree lighting. The huge fir stood in the center of the marketplace. Volunteers put last decorations in place. Sabrina had seen bigger trees than this one, though it dwarfed the small stands of the Christmas market surrounding it. Vendors were just opening, the place starting to come alive with the scents of various foods, chocolate, warm spices, and the ever-present pine.

Sabrina hadn't dreamed about the train, or anything Christmas-related, in a few days. The present moment still had that dream-like quality, making it feel like time was falling away, and with it, all adult responsibilities. Paying the bills, sharing her career with dedicated fans, representing her community, or trying to...

She walked past the Van Owens' stand. The family had been selling nutcrackers and Christmas pyramids had been here for generations. Sabrina's parents had bought a Christmas pyramid, and it stood in the living room each year. Watching the carousel turn from the warmth of the candles was another cherished childhood memory.

Another stand offered different varieties of gingerbread, eggnog, mulled wine, and other adult beverages guaranteed to keep visitors warm. The cheese fondue was new. Sabrina shook her head at herself when her stomach started growling—breakfast wasn't that long ago.

"It's as charming as ever, isn't it?"

She spun around, seeing her own surprise reflected on the man's face.

"Ethan! I didn't expect to meet you here of all places."

They had attended high school together. The last thing Sabrina had heard was that Ethan Donovan's family had moved away from Boxwood around the same time she left for L.A.

"It's not where I thought I'd see Sabrina Russell either. How are you?" he asked.

"Oh, I'm good, just taking a break from it all."

"Well, if that's what you're after, Boxwood is still a pretty good place. It's too bad it might change soon."

"I've heard it's the last year for the Christmas train."

"Yeah, your parents would be pretty disappointed. I'm afraid they'd be disappointed in me as well, but business is business, right? The numbers don't lie."

Sabrina had trouble hiding her confusion.

"Misty and Lori have done all they could. Dennis and Lorna would have loved them."

"How do you know Misty and Lori? We're talking about the same people, right? The Duncans?"

"Yes, of course." It was his turn to look surprised. "I realize...We never talked about this. It's been a long time since you came to Boxwood."

"So everyone keeps telling me."

"Listen, why don't we sit down for lunch and catch up? I was sure you knew I invested in the inn. It seemed like a good idea after the Connors left. Of course, we couldn't know what the future would bring."

"We never do, do we?" Sabrina asked wistfully. "I'd love to hear more though."

"Sure. How about a good old-fashioned stew at the Holden's?"

The temperature and the subjects they were going to discuss called for comfort food, so Sabrina agreed.

They went inside the Holden family's restaurant where one of the daughters, Mary, saw them to a table. After they'd chosen their meals, Ethan Donovan admitted, "I hate to bring this news to them before Christmas, but I have to protect my assets. Overall, the town has seen fewer tourists over the years, and the locals find it romantic but highly inconvenient on so many levels. I think if we sell now, we'll still get a fair price. Don't look so sad, Sabrina. Many things change."

"Oh, I'm aware." Sad wasn't the right word to describe her sudden and tumultuous emotions. If Ethan wanted to sell the inn, would Misty have no choice but to go along?

She had hoped to clear the sale with her and Lori and move on. Ethan's plans made a difference. She had to act fast.

"I'm sure. But let's not talk boring business matters. How's the high life in L.A.?"

"It's all right. I'd like to go back to what you said for a moment...Do you have a buyer already?"

"Not yet. I'm working on it, but I'm sure I'll find someone. It's a prime location. I also wanted to give Misty a heads-up first."

"That would be the fair thing to do. What would my parents' house go for these days?" Sabrina tried to keep her tone casual.

"Not as much as you'd think, but then again, it's been a buyer's market for a while. Boxwood isn't L.A., my dear."

Having just started her meal, Sabrina remembered why she hadn't always wanted to keep in touch...but it was hard to hide that they had a similar, privileged background. Current times weren't so easy for many people. Ethan Donovan could sell with a loss, and he'd still be fine. She needed him on her side, but Sabrina decided on a whim that it wasn't the right time to share her idea.

If he had the decency to talk to Misty first, she'd have to do the same.

Tonight, right after the tree-lighting.

·♥·♥·♥·♥·♥·

Sabrina hadn't seen Misty all day. She assumed with Ethan in town and complicated business decisions ahead, she was busy. Perhaps it wouldn't be all that bad. Misty understood how much this place meant to her, and most importantly, that she didn't mean to hurt her. They might be able to help each other.

A crowd had already gathered for the tree-lighting, and she tried not to jostle people too much while looking for Misty and Lori.

"Excuse me. I'm sorry."

"Sabrina. There you are."

She turned to Edie who gave her a bright smile. "Just like the old days when you were a little kid, right?"

"Almost. Have you seen Misty?"

"Over there."

From the other side of the square, Misty waved, and Sabrina hurried to go over to her side. She pulled her into a brief embrace, distantly aware of the conversations around them halting. When she stepped back, Misty's cheeks had reddened, though this time, Sabrina chalked it up to the temperature. It was freezing tonight.

"Hey. I'm here. What's going to happen?"

Misty smiled, and all of a sudden, it didn't seem so cold anymore.

"The same thing that happens every year. Except..."

The carol rose as if from out of nowhere. Sabrina hadn't noticed the choir on the balcony of the townhouse, but she was aware of it now, the rendition of *The First Noel* stirring up an emotion she hadn't been able to touch on yet.

After the song, Mayor Alicia Gaines took the stage and greeted the residents of Boxwood.

"Welcome to the annual tree-lighting! Here in Boxwood, we know how important it is to keep traditions alive," she continued, "and I'm so happy to see so many of you here. We also have a couple of surprises tonight, one of which you were just treated to."

Applause for the choir sounded again, making her smile.

"Yes, that was beautiful. And so is our tree, once again decorated by kind volunteers. Normally, I would get right to it, but that brings me to my other surprise. Not only will the lovely Sabrina Russell join me tonight, but she will be the one to switch on the lights. Welcome, Sabrina!"

It might not be entirely fair that she got more cheers than the choir or the volunteers since her task was such an easy one. In this case, Sabrina assumed the means justified the end.

There had to be a lesson, something to take away from the recent disappointments. She might rediscover her home. It might all be for the greater good.

She joined Mayor Gaines on the stage, seeking out Misty in the crowd. The way she looked at her with pride made Sabrina's heart beat faster. Sabrina admitted to herself that she regretted stepping back at the last moment. She desperately wanted a solution that would keep Misty in her life.

Everything was possible at Christmas, wasn't it?

"Hello, everyone," she said. "I'm so happy to be here! It's been a long time since I attended the annual tree lighting, and I'm thrilled that this time, I've actually been handed the switch." She held up the device, smiling brightly as she held Misty's gaze.

Here, with her, in her hometown, it had become easy to smile again. Not for cameras, not to be polite, but because it was in her heart.

"All right, let's do this. Ten...nine...eight..."

A joyful crowd counted with her.

"...three...two...one!"

She flipped the switch, and a multitude of tiny lights made the tree shine in all its glory, reflecting off of the many ornaments, an awe-inspiring sight that drew everyone's attention. Snowflakes were dancing in the wind.

"Thank you so much, Sabrina." The mayor gave her a quick hug before Sabrina stepped down to catch up with Misty whose eyes were shiny. Sabrina's had welled up a bit as well at this merging of past and present, childhood memories mingling with the more adult excitement she felt at this moment. Christmas time in Boxwood had never lost its magic.

And she could play a role in keeping an important part of it alive.

The choir launched into another song while residents still admired the tree, others went on their way to purchase treats and crafts from the Christmas market.

As they listened to the song, and then another, she felt Misty reaching for her hand, gently squeezed it back. They needed to talk, but it could wait a few more minutes. First, she needed a nice mug of mulled wine and something sweet.

Chapter Nine

Sabrina had noticed the man earlier. Judging from his camera, he was likely a reporter. She knew this was going to happen, part of her role to draw attention and funds to Boxwood. She didn't mind after having dealt with actual, uninvited transgressions.

"This was beautiful," she said to Misty as they walked along the stands of the Christmas market, admiring glass and wood creations.

"It is. At least no one can take that away from Boxwood."

"What do you mean?"

"Lori heard that our investor is coming to town. We're not sure why. He hasn't been around much since we all signed the contract." Misty shrugged. "It might not mean anything, but I think he put in that money on a whim. Perhaps he didn't know what to realistically expect from a town like Boxwood. He could take it away again."

He was about to...So Donovan hadn't talked to her yet, and she didn't even know he was already in town. Why? What was his deal? Sabrina couldn't imagine he didn't know what he had gotten himself into. After all, he'd grown up in Boxwood too.

"Would that be such a horrible thing in the long run?" Sabrina cringed at the surprise in Misty's expression. "I mean you said it yourself. No one knows what's going to happen once the train stops running, right?"

"Sure, but that's not a reason to give up. Besides, Lori and I have put everything into this. Our lives are here. We have nothing to fall back on."

There might have been a small jibe in that sentence, but Misty's tone didn't reflect it, so Sabrina decided not to dwell. In fact, she had an idea. She'd have to talk to Ethan again before she could share it with Misty...but it might just work if he wasn't interested in maintaining a small-town business. There was a chance each of them could get out of it what they hoped for.

"You'd just need another investor instead," she suggested.

"You say that like it's an easy thing to achieve."

"I don't know, it might be. Let's focus on the train for a moment...The booth at the tree lighting raised more money than we imagined."

"Yes, but..."

"We have to find a way to come up with more. If we can save the train, we won't have to worry about the inn."

"We," Misty repeated, sounding pensive and hopeful.

"Yes, we. I'm all in, remember?"

Sabrina hadn't expected Misty's arms around her the next moment, but she didn't mind, grateful they were on the same page. For the most part, anyway. She held on, remembering the moment on the ice rink once more. Some difficult conversations still lay ahead, but she felt a little more confident about handling them. She couldn't wait for the next time they were alone together, a moment when they wouldn't have to talk business or raising money.

By Christmas, at the latest.

All in.

"There you are." Lori's voice startled them apart. "Who's ready for some mulled wine?"

·♥·♥·♥·♥·♥·

At times, it was still unreal to Misty that the woman who had occupied her thoughts for so long, was here in Boxwood, mobilizing an effort to not only save the Christmas train, but keep the inn in her and Lori's hands for the foreseeable future. Whatever the outcome of either one would be, one thing was for sure: Within a few days, Sabrina had come to mean so much more to her than a celebrity crush.

If she told her, would that make a difference? Sabrina seemed so much at home here, but would that still be true without the magic of the holidays? Did she have enough of a reason to stay?

"Okay Santa," she said out loud. "It's already been amazing. Is it greedy if I still want more?"

"I don't think it is," Lori who had just walked into the kitchen, said. "But you might want to take a look at this. It's not good."

"What do you mean? Did Mayor Gaines say anything?"

"It's not the mayor," Lori said cryptically. "Were we really that naive?"

She handed Misty a copy of the *Holbrooke Herald*. As Misty started to read the article, she could feel her jaw drop, her hopeful musings drowned out by a sense of unease. No, dread was more like it.

Boxwood Native Sabrina Russell Returns To Purchase Her Childhood Home.

"Did you know about this?" Lori asked. Demanded was more like it. "Look, I know you like her, but I thought the inn was for the long run. For the retirement fund."

"Wait, no, I didn't know about it. You know I would never sell the inn!" Misty continued to read, feeling worse with each second. There was no way Sabrina had decided this spontaneously. Had her interest in Misty simply been a pretense? "She hinted that there might be a way to get another investor if Donovan dropped out…I don't understand this. Why didn't he come to us first?"

"Perhaps because he likes her as a buyer? Question is, why didn't she tell us right away?" Lori pointed out the obvious and painful.

"People write a lot about her. It doesn't mean that she's going to kick us out. She knows we have nowhere to go." If she sounded panicked, it reflected her state of mind perfectly.

"Well, it doesn't look like she has a lot of options either. Wow."

Misty couldn't bring herself to believe that Sabrina's display of kindness, and her contributions for Boxwood and its charming traditions had been for one reason only. There had to be an explanation. She continued reading.

After her career took a few hits, Ms. Russell returned to her hometown and childhood home, and met with investor Ethan Donovan. Like Boxwood's Christmas Train, Misty's Maison Inn *could soon be a thing of the past…*

"No."

Sources say that Ms. Russell has returned to Boxwood for good, after Hollywood turned its back on her: After some quick successes, the studio indefinitely shelved her self-funded movie, deciding it wasn't a good fit for them. She also recently lost a few roles to younger, less political competitors.

"A few?" Misty cringed when she realized her voice had gone up a notch. "It was one role! She wanted to take a break. She didn't even know that the house was now a B&B."

"Well, you can ask her," Lori said with a pointed look to the door when they both heard the knock.

Misty folded the newspaper and laid it on the counter behind her.

"Come on in."

"Sorry I'm so late," Sabrina said with a smile. "I might have a little too much of that mulled wine last night. It was delicious though."

"It's not a problem."

Misty hesitated, aware of Lori's gaze on her. With Christmas this close, it was probably a good idea to clear the air right away, even if everyone's livelihood depended on the outcome. She couldn't stand to be left in the dark any longer.

"Sabrina, there's something we need to talk about—"

"I really look forward to the train—" Sabrina said at the same time, and they shared an awkward laugh, falling silent afterwards.

"Okay, if you won't do it, I will," Lori declared. "Sabrina, did you come here to buy this house out from under us?"

"What? No." Sabrina's denial was swift, to Misty's relief. She sighed, before she pulled herself a chair and sat. "It's true though, there is something we'll have to talk about."

"So talk. We're listening."

"Lori," Misty chided, uncomfortable with her sister's harsh tone.

"Don't worry about it, Misty. I probably deserved that, and I'm really sorry I didn't say anything earlier. I was aware people were going to talk about...what happened, back in L.A." Sabrina paused as if searching for words, regret written all over her face. "I came here with a lot of doubts, about myself, about who I even am," she continued. "I thought that the Connors might be interested in selling, and if I moved back here, into this house, I could connect to the person I was, the life I had here."

"But the Connors aren't here anymore," Lori prompted.

"No. Instead you have welcomed me without questions, and I am so grateful for that. I can't blame you if you don't believe me, but that made it much harder. I didn't lie to you. I really want to help where I can. I've loved the past few days so much, everything we did. I wish..." She gazed at Misty, unmistakable longing in her expression. She didn't finish her sentence. Instead, she said, "Ethan and I went to high school together. I swear, until yesterday, I had no idea he was even involved in the inn."

"How did you imagine this was going to work? When were you going to tell us?" Misty asked. She wasn't sure how to feel about any of it. She was aware that Sabrina, too, was conflicted. She had questions for her she didn't want to raise in Lori's presence. Never mind the much more pressing answers they needed.

"Soon. I thought that if I could work something out with him, you and I could find a solution together, but Ethan doesn't want to sell his assets to me. All that bad press has him worried I couldn't pay, so he declined. He said he'll make a final decision after the holidays, but if that involves another buyer, I don't know. I swear."

"Well, I guess then I'm sorry for all of us, and we need some more coffee," Lori declared. "All of it happened this morning?" There was still a hint of suspicion to her tone.

"I ran into him the other day, then I made some calls and made the offer this morning. I'm sorry it's not enough. I so wanted to help. But maybe it's for the better. Honestly, I don't know anymore."

"Like I said, more coffee first."

Lori all but jumped into action, while Misty was still stunned by the turn of events. While the coffee was brewing, Lori's phone rang, and she excused herself, leaving Sabrina and Misty in an awkward silence only interrupted by the sounds of the coffeemaker.

"What's going to happen next?" she wondered out loud. Misty didn't have an answer, and if she was honest, she didn't expect Sabrina to have one either.

"I can talk to him again if you want," Sabrina offered. "Honestly? I don't know what I was thinking. If this had still been a one-family home, if the Connors were still here, I might have been able to work something out, but I don't think the bank will be on board with me investing in a business at this moment. It looks like I'll have to face some unpleasant truths...but Misty, that doesn't mean you and Lori will be out of your home. Ethan might be short-sighted when it comes to the potential of small towns, but not everyone is."

"So, you're getting on the next flight back?" Misty asked, unable to keep the bitterness out of her tone.

"No, of course not! I still want to spend Christmas here, even if I'm a guest. Boxwood is my home, and you..."

That moment, Lori returned to the kitchen, her expression unreadable.

Again, Sabrina abandoned whatever it was she wanted to say.

"That was the mayor," Lori said. "I told her she can still count on seeing you on the train?"

That was meant for Sabrina.

"Of course. I..." She cast an uncertain glance at Misty. "We're all going, right? Whatever happens, you have gone out of your way to make Christmas amazing, and I want that for all of us."

81

Lori's expression softened some. "Well, you and Misty will go. Someone will have to keep the business open, and I sure don't mind doing it."

"Again, I'm so sorry. I thought that if Ethan had said yes..." She shook her head.

"What's done is done," Lori declared. "We know one thing for sure. The train is going to run as planned this year, and according to Mayor Gaines, it's going to be a huge success. It would have been easier on all of us if you had told us first, but we'll work this out."

When she caught Sabrina's hopeful glance on her, Misty wanted to believe.

It was Christmas after all.

"Let's try," she said.

Chapter Ten

Things had happened fast. Whether the reporter who had written the story did or didn't mean to call her credit into question, the result stayed the same: Ethan had quickly declined her offer, saying he'd delay until after the holidays when he'd try to find someone more affluent.

If he did, there was no saying what would happen to *Misty's Maison Inn*. Sabrina had woefully overestimated her small-town-saving abilities, carried away by the same illusions that led her to believe she could be a powerful force for good. A Christmas delusion rather than a miracle, but at least they still had a few days together.

Her vision blurred as she stood in front of the Christmas tree in the lobby, her gaze falling on the old ornament hanging on the tree. When Sabrina sold to the Connors, she didn't think she was ever going to come back, let alone celebrate Christmas in this house. She had taken a few personal things and then all but fled.

In the past few days, it had felt more like a home than any apartment or condo she'd had in L.A. It was Misty's home too.

"We found those in a box in the attic," Misty had appeared behind her.

"I didn't know the Connors kept them. Some of those are really old."

The miniature version of the Christmas train's old-fashioned locomotive she had spotted on her first day, decorated in red, green, and silver glitter, with the year it had been sold. There were a few others, glass spheres in various colors, an angel, a Santa Claus.

"And this one, I made," Sabrina said with a wistful smile, remembering when her clay creation first made an appearance.

"Really? It's so cute. We have put all of them on the tree, every year." They both regarded the decorations in silence, until Misty asked softy, "Are you ready?"

All in all, the conversation could have gone much worse for either of them. There was no doubt they were still a bit shaken. Misty believed that Sabrina never meant to do any harm. It mattered to her above all. Sabrina would stay for the holidays. Would it give them enough time to figure out what they both wanted from the future? She wasn't sure, but today, Misty wasn't going to dwell—much.

"As ready as I'll ever be," Sabrina answered. "Let's go."

As promised, Lori would hold down the fort for the day, while they went to set up things for the toy drive.

The organizers assigned them a table where they worked side by side, accepting toy donations and money that would go directly to a women's shelter a bit further out of town, and local families.

Sabrina noticed a girl, about ten years old, who was dropping off a box of toys with her mother.

"Wow, that is very generous of you to give all of those to children who don't have any toys. What's your name?" The girl looked down to her feet.

"It's Emma," her mother supplied. "I don't let her see all your movies yet, but she loves the ones that were okay for her age. Would it be too annoying if I asked you to sign a poster for her?"

"Oh no, it's not a problem at all. You know, I was really shy when I was younger," she said, smiling at the girl. "Acting helped me to get over it."

"Thank you," Emma said, beaming, as she received the signed poster.

"Thank you so much, and Merry Christmas," her mother added.

"Merry Christmas."

Sabrina was aware of Misty's gaze on her.

"I should have come back much sooner," she said wistfully. "And I'm glad I can help make someone's Christmas a little brighter. I'm still so sorry I ruined yours."

Misty laid a hand on her arm. "You didn't ruin anything. It's still not your fault."

"That doesn't make a difference, does it?"

"Tonight, we'll go on the train. After that...we'll see."

A few more people politely asked for autographs. One teenage girl with a blue streak in her hair awkwardly clutched her cell phone, so Sabrina offered to take a selfie together.

The girl said a quick thank you and all but fled from the scene. Sabrina had seen her eyes well up.

"I can't thank you enough," Paula, one of the organizers she had met at the Christmas committee, said. "You too, Misty. The guests at the inn are always generous."

"Thank you," Misty replied. "I know that we're not pulling as many attendees as our star guest though. I'm grateful Sabrina is here."

"We all are. We already collected over twice as much money as last year, and the Christmas train is sold out. The company might not change their mind, but we can sure show them we value this tradition, and it's something beautiful for children and adults."

"It's a shame. This is...It was special," Sabrina agreed, her throat going tight. It seemed like whenever she thought there was a sliver of hope, it was taken away the next moment. She couldn't continue like this. She needed to start living in the moment rather than an imaginary future or a safer past. "But I'll get to see it one more time, with new friends I made, so I'm grateful for that."

"We're happy to have you here, Sabrina."

She had to believe that they really meant it. Because she wanted to find a way to stay.

·♥·♥·♥·♥·♥·

For the town of Boxwood, it would be the best Christmas in some time. Misty couldn't ignore the warm feeling of hope, given what they had already achieved on this day. An unexpected amount of money and toys would go to the shelter and struggling families of Boxwood. That wasn't nothing. It was something to be grateful for.

Something else she found impossible to ignore—Sabrina's excitement when they left the venue to walk to the train station where they'd board the Christmas train. Passengers had assigned seats, so no one would be standing.

Misty couldn't remember the last time she had seen so many people interested in the ride. Sabrina's self-confidence might have taken a hit with recent experiences, but she had to acknowledge that her presence had made a big difference for many people around here.

A few days before her arrival, most of them had shrugged and said, "all good things come to an end." Misty had been almost ready to believe it, but what if they could convince Donovan to give them another chance? What if the train could continue to be Boxwood's cherished Christmas tradition?

What if Sabrina didn't leave?

Once they arrived on the platform, she realized that already more people were waiting than the train would hold. Many had simply come for the last farewell. Among others, *The Dining Car* and Holden's provided visitors with snacks from their restaurants, and there were booths with sweet treats and hot beverages as well.

She could sense Sabrina's mixed emotions, and it was only natural she'd take her hand. Sabrina held hers tightly in return.

"Thank you for sharing this with me," she whispered.

"My pleasure," Misty said, smiling. Sabrina held her gaze for a long time, until the train's whistle startled them back out of the possibilities, and into reality.

Chapter Eleven

"I can't believe it! It's exactly like I remember."

Sabrina wished she could get a handle on all those emotions to read her life clearly and find what she was supposed to do. She still felt a deep melancholy regarding the last times she'd been on the train, a bit older than in those dreams—but she wasn't alone.

Misty was with her, her gaze on Sabrina warm and calm even though she was going through some turmoil of her own.

"Good evening. What can I bring you? Oh. Wow. It's so great to have you here, Ms. Russell."

For a few seconds she'd been drawn deep into the past, amazed that even the waitress's uniform was the same. But Sabrina was an adult now, perhaps with enough fame to her name to make a difference.

Could she turn her own life around?

"I'd like a hot chocolate with whipped cream," she said. "Misty, the same for you?"

"Sure."

"You'd like me to add a little shot of Irish cream liquor?" the waitress asked.

Sabrina almost laughed. She certainly did not remember that question, not for her anyway, though she remembered her parents had had the occasional eggnog on this train. "Why not? It's a special occasion."

"This must have been amazing for you as a child. I can only imagine, all the lights and decorations."

Sabrina laughed softly. "Yes, and thinking you're really good doing Santa a favor, so he has time to deliver all the presents."

"That is such a cute obfuscation."

"And I believed it too, for a long time." Sabrina leaned back into the booth, thinking the interior of the train must have been renovated since those days. "Lori told me you've had some pretty magical Christmases as well."

"Oh yes." Misty's smile deepened. "No matter what happened during the year, if we struggled with anything, had to find new friends, all that went away during this time. Our parents always made it special."

"They sound like great people."

"They were," Misty confirmed. "And I think they'd be happy that we found a permanent home, though I'm not so sure anymore how long that will last."

"All isn't lost yet. Look at how many people came. Mayor Gaines will have a point to make to the company, and Ethan...he might still come around."

Outside, people were waving and cheering as the whistle announced the departure of the train.

"Maybe," Misty agreed. She didn't sound one hundred percent convinced, and Sabrina didn't blame her. Much was still up in the air, but that wouldn't keep them from enjoying this special moment.

The waitress came to bring their order, and they clinked their mugs together. The first sip of the sweet alcoholic beverage went straight to her head. As the train left the station, Sabrina's memory was as clear as the dreams had been. She wasn't a child any longer, but an adult who was able to see things in a different light. Her parents had enjoyed bringing her on this yearly adventure, what it meant to her...It had meant a lot to them as a couple too. She could remember the smiles they shared. The unspoken affection.

She held Misty's gaze thinking that there was no one she'd rather share this with in the present.

She reached out to take her hand, and Misty didn't pull back. The magical ride, through snow-covered field and forests, with the view of houses welcoming Christmas, continued.

Perhaps she'd never really arrived in the present until recently. Sabrina found that she didn't want to go back any longer. There was too much to do, to experience, in the here and now.

·♥·♥·♥·♥·♥·

The train picked up passengers at the destination stop before it made the way back to Boxwood. Misty didn't want it to end, though she knew that sometime soon, they would have to face reality, regarding the end of an era, maybe of the inn.

Some time after the holidays, Sabrina would certainly have to go back to L.A. to resume her career, which meant for Misty...She sighed.

"Hey. Don't feel bad. I think we did everything we could drawing attention to this issue. Now people will have to decide."

"Yes, I guess they will," she said. "I'm glad you enjoyed it. That must have brought up a lot of memories."

"You're right, it did. But mostly I'm glad that I got to do this again now, as an adult. When you're a happy, spoiled child..."

Sabrina laughed self-consciously. "And it's very obvious to me now that that's what I was...The world revolves around you. I didn't realize how romantic this was until now."

Now she was just twisting the knife.

"You're finding inspiration for your next movie?"

"Maybe that's not what I need inspiration for." Sabrina held her gaze, now serious. "It's not even realistic right now that I could do my own thing, and I didn't come here for professional reasons. Maybe it's in another area that I need inspiration, and you're right, I'm finding it."

Misty felt her face heat, the way it always did when it sounded like Sabrina was flirting with her. Like this was at all realistic, even though she was long past the stage of celebrity crush. Misty had been falling for her since the moment she'd walked up to the counter of *Misty's Maison Inn*, a bit more every day since she got to know the woman behind the persona.

Perhaps it was for the best that Sabrina would leave. It might be the reality check Misty needed—and it was what she most feared, more than any of the difficult decisions ahead.

"Either way, that's a good thing," she responded vaguely.

"It is."

At the Boxwood train station there were still people to greet the train, even though it stopped here. Misty cast a quick glance at Sabrina, wondering if she had the same sense of finality. It had to be worse when it meant so much to her.

Sabrina, however, was all smiles as she shook hands and took pictures, her cheeks flushed from the cold.

What if Donovan did change his mind? Maybe she and Sabrina could work together...make a home together? She shook her head. It had to be the alcohol in the hot chocolate.

"Ready to go home?" Sabrina asked, and Misty realized that the small crowd had dispersed. It was starting to snow again.

"I guess I am. Let's go."

They walked past the Christmas market where vendors were about to close, and towards the inn.

It looked beautiful illuminated by Christmas lights, Misty thought, her breath catching in her throat. To Lori's chagrin, she had gotten on the roof to make sure every lightbulb was in the right place. Their business, and home. A fresh coat of snow in the front yard made everything look clean, the decorations thoughtful and inviting.

To Sabrina, it was a temporary place to stay and her childhood home that held all those magical memories.

They walked up to the apartment in silence. Time to say goodnight.

"I'll see you tomorrow? We're going to have a party for the guests later. It would be great if you could come...not just for publicity," Misty corrected herself hastily. "I'd love to see you there."

"I will be there," Sabrina promised. "Thank you for tonight. I know things are still complicated, but I appreciate it so much. It was everything I could have hoped for."

"Of course. It was my pleasure."

They both hesitated for a few heartbeats before Sabrina said, "I know there's no mistletoe here..." She didn't finish her sentence, but instead leaned in to kiss Misty softly. For a split-second, Misty stood frozen until she allowed herself to realize that this was happening. She wasn't dreaming. And finally, she returned the warm, tender act, her mind racing. *Does she really mean this?* What did it mean?

What now?

When she stepped back, there was a sparkle in Sabrina's eyes. She looked incredibly beautiful.

"I'm so glad no one interrupted us. I've been wanting to do this for a long time. Good night, Misty," Sabrina said, her tone lighter and happier than Misty had ever heard it. "And Merry Christmas."

"Merry Christmas, Sabrina."

When the door closed, Misty turned around to go to her own apartment, her heart racing all of a sudden. She touched her lips, reminding herself that this time it wasn't a dream. She hadn't made it up. Sabrina had kissed her. She hadn't asked her inside.

Misty had to admit she wasn't ready for anything more at this moment, though her imagination was as usual far ahead. This wasn't the end. It simply would have been too strange for Sabrina to invite her into the bedroom that her parents had shared before.

"Crazy. I'm crazy," she muttered to herself as she let herself into the apartment, walking straight into the kitchen where she yelped. "Lori, what are you doing sitting in the dark?"

Lori shrugged and smiled. "Watching the snow fall. It's relaxing. I'm also watching who's coming and going...So you had a good time?"

"Oh. Yes. There were so many people. If that doesn't convince Donovan that we're not over yet, nothing will."

"That prospect has you really excited," Lori observed.

"Of course. It's our home, our livelihood."

"But that's not the only thing you're excited about. You took quite some time to get here. Will you finally admit I was right all along?"

"I'm not sure I'm willing to do that just yet. There's a lot to figure out. But...we kissed." Misty was a tad embarrassed about blurting it out like a teenager. Saying it out loud made it more real, and she needed that.

"That's wonderful! I know I've been hard on her, but I believe she's really trying to make up for her mistake. She's a good person. I'm so happy for you."

"Could you hold back just a little bit?" Misty pleaded. "We haven't talked a lot, not about this. "I don't know where it's going, or if it's going anywhere at all. Sabrina will have to go back to L.A. at some point."

"Could you imagine going with her, then?"

"What? Stop it!"

Lori shrugged, unfazed by her reaction.

"First of all, I wouldn't leave you all alone with the business, but aside from that, did you listen to me? It was one kiss."

"One kiss that has you glowing, sis. A good beginning, I'd say."

"Whatever you say. I'm going to bed now. Tomorrow's going to be a long day."

"Misty! Wait a second. It's Christmas Eve, remember?"

Misty halted her step, embarrassed. "Of course. I'm so sorry. Even if it's a little bit your fault."

"I'll gladly take the blame," Lori returned, her amusement obvious. "You didn't want to see your gift?"

"I do. Just let me get yours, okay?"

She went to get the box she had hidden on the top shelf of her closet a couple of weeks ago. When Misty returned, Lori had retreated to the living room, and she had a plate of cookies and two hot chocolates ready.

"How did you do that so fast? It's like…"

"Magic? I've been ready. It's what we always do."

"Now I feel even worse…"

It was true, tonight Misty had forgotten about all but the joy in Sabrina's eyes when she got to relive a precious childhood memory. Her smile, full of promise, after their kiss.

"Please. Don't. But I want to see what's in that box right now."

"Of course. Merry Christmas."

Lori's face lit up when she opened her present and revealed the stack of romance novels Misty had chosen for her.

"How did you even know I wanted this one...Thank you so much!"

Misty hugged her tightly. "I shouldn't reveal my tactics, but let's just say your wish lists were easy to find."

"I'm so glad. And I might miss work sometime in the future because I can't wait to get to them. Thank you. Now let's see what Santa brought for you." She went over to the tree and retrieved a box of her own. "Whatever Sabrina decides, I'm sure you'll have an occasion for this."

Misty opened the lid. She could feel her jaw drop when she took out the red dress, something more daring—and certainly more expensive—than she would have ever bought for herself.

"Lori! This is...It's so kind of you, but this is too much."

"No, it's not," her sister objected. "Every year, you work so hard to make everyone, including me, happy. I know you've been dreaming about something big to happen, well, it is happening. Sabrina cares about you. You're dating a star now, might as well dress the part."

Misty shook her head, still baffled. "That cost a lot more than the gift I gave you."

"It's not about that. You know I love my gift. And, well, you could wear this tomorrow."

It might be more appropriate for a romantic dinner than the annual party with guests and family, but she couldn't deny she liked that idea.

"It's beautiful. Thank you."

"You're welcome."

Misty took a sip of her hot chocolate, barely suppressing a yawn. "Tonight was really beautiful. The Christmas train, and this inn, mean so much, not just to us, but the people here."

"And Sabrina."

"And Sabrina," she confirmed.

"I believe in happy endings, sis. They can be for us, too."

As she looked outside the window, where the snow was falling softly, neighbor's Christmas lights twinkling in the distance, Misty was willing to believe too. It was Christmas after all, and tomorrow, she'd get to celebrate her favorite holiday with the woman she had fallen in love with. Who said miracles didn't happen?

Chapter Twelve

Nothing had turned out the way she'd planned, and yet...Sabrina couldn't bring herself to worry much. She had spent years worrying, about whether she was good enough for her chosen profession, whether she'd be able to make a difference in anyone's life. A lot of people here in Boxwood still believed she could, believed in her.

Most of all...Misty.

She was a fan, had said so herself. She didn't have any knowledge of the field, or whatever Sabrina's life behind the scenes looked like, and usually that would have been a red flag. This was different, *they* were different here in Boxwood. The way she made Sabrina feel, was real too.

She couldn't wait for the next day, Christmas Day, when she could kiss her again, perhaps under mistletoe this time. Taking it slow...Sabrina laughed softly, knowing that there was no way she could have invited Misty into her parents' old bedroom, given all the implications. They had time. Maybe for the first time of her life, she didn't feel rushed. They might have to move a bit faster to find solutions for Misty's business, but the pace at which their new friendship was evolving into something different, was entirely up to them.

She closed her eyes with a smile on her face. Her therapist would be proud, though Sabrina didn't feel like she'd done all that much, except for taking a chance when it presented itself. The rest was Christmas magic.

.♥.♥.♥.♥.♥.

The next morning, she sought out Misty, glad to realize that Lori wasn't present. Sabrina liked her direct, no-nonsense ways, but she wanted to spend some time alone with Misty before any other social interaction.

"Good morning," she said, entering the apartment and the kitchen after a quick knock.

Misty stood at the stove, preparing pancake batter from the looks of it. Her face lit up when she saw Sabrina.

"Hey. You're up early."

"Couldn't sleep. Too excited."

Misty's smile widened. "For presents?"

"Among other things, yes." When Sabrina leaned in, Misty eagerly met her halfway. Their kiss was as sweet and tender as the first one. After a few heartbeats, it might have easily turned into something more passionate, as Lori walked in.

"Good morning, my lovelies. Don't mind me."

"I mind a little," Misty said as Sabrina took a seat, "but that's okay."

"So, Sabrina, you're coming to the Christmas party today."

"Of course. I wouldn't miss it."

Lori poured them some coffee and sat down with her mug.

"I have talked to a few people, and all of them said that the town feels different. There haven't been that many passengers, or those greeting the train in years. You might be our saving grace."

"I didn't really do anything except show my face," Sabrina said, feeling wistful. "I wish I could change Donovan's mind on the inn."

"There might be a chance, still," Lori said. "I invited him to the party, and he said he'd stop by."

The ladle cluttered to the floor, batter splattering onto the hardwood floor.

"You did what?" Misty asked, obviously not in the loop.

Sabrina stood up to get a rag to clean up the floor. She was intrigued as well.

"He's happy to participate in the Secret Santa. I think that's a good sign."

"Wow. Okay." Misty cleaned the ladle and put it on the counter.

"It is," Lori insisted. "He can see for himself how we run things here, and that the inn is a good, important thing for Boxwood, and its traditions. He knows Sabrina, so he must have some idea."

Sabrina sat back down as well. "To be honest, I'm not sure how much that's worth to him, because he's looking at the bottom line first and foremost. But we have something to show for. You're still booked solid, donations at the toy drive have been at an all-time high, and the train was a success. He won't ignore that."

Misty gave her an affectionate smile. Her tone was more sober.

"If only we had one more investor, that would convince him." She turned back to her pan, before she put the first pancake onto Sabrina's plate. Lori watched with an expression that showed her amusement, and not for Misty's words.

In her mind, Sabrina went over the days she'd spent here, the people she'd met. It was hard to imagine what would convince Ethan if the benefit for the community didn't.

But perhaps she had one more ace up her sleeve. She didn't want to promise too much to Misty and Lori and risk another disappointment.

"Let's hope you're right," Lori said. "Now let's eat. We'll have a lot to do today."

·♥·♥·♥·♥·♥·

Nevertheless, they found a private moment for themselves after Lori had left to talk to a delivery man. All of a sudden, Misty was beyond nervous.

"Relax," Sabrina advised. "It will all be fine."

"That's yet to be determined," Misty mumbled.

"I know it." Sabrina wrapped her arms around her, and Misty was more than eager to let herself be convinced. She couldn't stop herself.

"I'm glad. Is there...something else we should talk about?"

Sabrina brushed her fingertips over Misty's hair, making her shiver. "I'm really sorry for closing the door in your face, but that room, it's just too strange."

"I thought so. It wouldn't be the same for every room in this house, would it?" Misty asked, feeling her face flush with the obvious insinuation.

"I don't think so," Sabrina said, laughing, a warm happy sound that made Misty all happy and warm inside, too. "But as Lori said, there's a lot to do. We'll come back to that?"

"Sure." She didn't have the heart to ask the hard questions. *How much longer will you stay? Is this a good enough reason to stay? Am I?* Misty had a hard time believing that anyone would leave stardom behind for her, though she couldn't imagine her life without Sabrina anymore.

"We'll find some time for ourselves, I promise you. I like you, Misty. A lot."

That had to be enough to tide her over, though Misty wished they could just hide away from people and obligations today. She couldn't ignore the more pressing reality.

"I like you too, but I guess you figured that out the moment we met."

"Yes," Sabrina admitted. "Usually, people are less interested the longer I'm around them so...I'm hopeful. Let's just make this day the best it can be, and we'll go from there?"

"Yes. And thank you so much for everything. I appreciate it."

"I know."

This time, their kiss left no open questions.

·❤·❤·❤·❤·❤·

Later that morning, Sabrina helped with preparing the room for the party. Guests had signed up for the Secret Santa and put gifts under the tree. Sometime around noon, Sabrina cast a deliberate glance at her watch.

"Are you going to be okay? I have to run one more errand. I'll be back later for the Secret Santa...and your gift, of course."

She almost laughed when her rather innocent words made Misty blush. For the longest time, Sabrina hadn't considered herself such a gift, but flattery hurt no one. That, and her heart beat a bit faster now that she was considering the possibilities. All in good time. First, she had something else to take care of.

Fifteen minutes later she found herself at the counter of *The Dining Car*. They had been closed the night before but opened for lunch and dinner today.

"Sabrina! What can I do for you?" Edie's expression showed her surprise.

Perhaps she was getting ahead of herself, as in everything, but she wanted to know all the options before she took her next steps.

"I know you're busy, but I was hoping we could talk for a few minutes...There's something I'd like to run by you."

"Of course. You must be close to leaving town, for all the exciting adventures waiting for you?"

Edie obviously didn't care for tabloid gossip.

"I'm not sure yet when exactly that will be. For now, I'm glad to be in Boxwood and celebrating Christmas here."

"Yes. I'm surprised Misty isn't here."

Sabrina didn't think she needed to confirm or deny what Edie was saying between the lines.

"I'm getting straight to the point. You might have heard that Mr. Donovan is about to pull his investments from the inn. The results would be devastating for Misty and Lori, and I believe, in the long run, for Boxwood. The house, the connection to my family and the community, it matters."

"I agree, sweetheart." A smile lit up her face. "Wait a minute! Is that it? You're coming home for real?"

"I've been thinking about it. I wanted to invest in the inn, to keep it running, but unfortunately Ethan thinks I'm not creditworthy enough. You might have read those stories."

"That's rubbish. Because of one project and one role? There are still so many opportunities for you, here at home and in your career," Edie said with conviction.

"I'm glad you think so. It's just that my hands are tied a bit when it comes to big financial moves, so I was wondering...The restaurant is doing well, isn't it? I was hoping you could be the one to lend a hand to Misty."

When seconds ticked by and Edie still hadn't said anything, her expression apologetic, Sabrina knew she wasn't going to pull off a miracle today.

"I am sorry if this is a bad time."

"I'm afraid it is," Edie said, her regret showing in her posture. "The truth is, like most businesses in Boxwood, we're...good, I think. Relatively speaking. It's not a time where we can make big steps like that, much as I'd like to. The inn and your parents' memory mean a lot to us too. I'm so sorry, Sabrina."

"It's not your fault," she hurried to say, nevertheless touched at the mention of her parents. She wanted to honor their memory. The problem was every possible door was closing in her face, and time was running out.

"I know. I still wish there was something we could do in the long run."

"Me too." Sabrina sighed. "I don't know, maybe the Secret Santa will be a surprise, and someone has a few hundred grand to give?" Even better if that one was Ethan, though she doubted it. "Thank you for listening. I don't want to keep you any longer."

"It's not a problem. This is the least I could do. Have you had lunch yet?"

"No, not really." She also still had to wrap her gift and confess this last-ditch effort to Misty. Sabrina didn't mind stalling a bit on the latter, disappointed as she was with the results.

"Then you're invited. I have something to tell you," a cheery voice said behind her. "Wow, there you are finally. I had to travel to the middle of nowhere to find you."

That moment, Sabrina was sure she had to be dreaming. Whether it was a good dream or not, was yet to be determined.

Chapter Thirteen

Misty surveyed the room with a critical eye, glad every corner passed her inspection. The party would soon start. She felt like taking a nap, preferably until the next day, but the place would be full of guests within the next hour. Sabrina hadn't come back yet, and she was starting to worry.

Nothing bad happened in Boxwood. She had probably been held up by friendly residents or fans—or both. Everyone was aware that their good fortune of having Sabrina Russell in town might not last. She sighed, unaware that Lori had come up behind her.

"We've given this everything we could. And if this is our last Christmas here, it sure is as perfect as it can be," she said, and after a pause, "She's still not back?"

"No."

"Okay, don't make that face. You've seen what it's like. I'm sure she's doing selfies somewhere. She doesn't seem to mind, and no one's been too annoying."

"Yet."

"Come on, it's Christmas."

"Exactly," Misty returned, unwilling to hide her frustration. "Don't people have better things to do on a day like this?"

"You'd think."

They were both silent for a few seconds, before Misty said, "Would you be able to handle things by yourself for a bit? I'll make it quick."

"Of course." Lori's response was swift enough to tell Misty that she, too, was wondering what was going on. She went to get her coat and left, unsure where to go.

She considered going to the train station, but then stopped at *The Dining Car*. She was about to go in when she saw the two women sitting at the table by the window. The scene looked cozy with the Christmas decoration on the table. They had glasses of champagne in front of them.

Misty couldn't make sense of the scene any way. She knew she had to move, or someone would catch her staring. The other woman had shoulder-length dark hair. She looked familiar...Misty froze when she realized who she was. Had Sabrina left out a big part of the truth as to why she'd left L.A.? She said she'd been too busy to date. But what if someone had left her behind, like Abby had done it to Misty?

What if that person now wanted her back?

She backed away, aware that she couldn't base her next steps on her own insecurities—though there were few reasons why Emily Davis, who was at the height of her career, would follow Sabrina to Boxwood. Weren't there?

"Misty, wait!"

She had hesitated too long. Sabrina had appeared in the doorway. Reluctantly, Misty turned around.

"I'm sorry. You're busy and...I didn't mean to spy on you."

"Please come in. I'm sorry too, for leaving you with all the work. Emily and I had a lot to talk about."

Misty was fairly proud of herself when she didn't give a snippy response. Sabrina had the right to have lunch with a colleague. She, on the other hand, had no right or reason to be jealous.

"I could see that. She's come a long way to meet you."

"It's not like that," Sabrina said softly. "I still want to come to the party. In fact, let me just say goodbye and I'll join you?" She didn't wait for an answer, just walked back inside the restaurant. Misty had no choice but to wait.

She tried again when Sabrina came back out, now wearing her coat, hat, and scarf.

"You didn't have to leave like this."

"Oh, Emily won't mind. She's going to drive back to the airport. There's no way she's going to find a room tonight."

Misty almost had a guilty conscience for how relieved she felt at this.

"But even if she had, you might want to know Emily's straight." Sabrina couldn't quite keep a straight face saying it, and Misty had to smile as well.

"I'm that obvious?"

"I'm afraid so, but I'm the actress, so it's all good. I promise you, this is something good. Better than good."

"You're going to tell me? We have a bit of time before the party..."

"No, we don't. I still need to change. I swear, I'll tell you everything later."

Misty found no reason not to believe her, though she was curious. "I already know it was champagne worthy..."

"Yes. And we'll discuss it later." Sabrina saw through her tactics, and she ended the argument with a tender kiss. "Now let's go find out what the Secret Santa brought."

·♥·♥·♥·♥·♥·

Misty had little time to update Lori as some of the guests had already arrived, and she, too, still had to change.

"So, all is well?" Lori asked between directing staff and greeting more attendees.

Was it? Sabrina had assured her that there was no reason to worry.

And here she was, coming down the stairs in a dress that was definitely more than Boxwood formal—more classic Hollywood movie style.

"You're gaping." Lori chuckled. "Which I can kind of understand but remember you're not alone in the room."

"You're so funny. I'll be right back." Misty headed upstairs. She and Sabrina shared a smile, their fingers lightly touching as they passed each other by. She wanted to turn around and sneak another look, but she had to be quick now.

In record time, she took a quick shower and only hesitated for a heartbeat before she put on the dress Lori had bought for her. Misty dried her hair and wound it up in a loose bun, amazed at the transformation.

It was true, she had dreamed of a moment like this, even though she'd never expected it to happen under such complicated circumstances.

But they could still find a way, somehow.

When she stood on the landing a few minutes later, she allowed herself some time to watch Sabrina mingle with the other guests, a glass of champagne in hand. As if aware of her gaze, Sabrina looked up, a smile lighting up her face at the sight of Misty. She mouthed something that Misty read as "gorgeous." *Look who's talking.*

For the first time in months, a bit of the stress that had settled in her shoulders, left her.

DESTINATION CHRISTMAS, NEXT STOP LOVE

Merry Christmas, Misty thought. Whatever happened from now on, she promised she'd follow her heart, with no regrets. She went back downstairs to join their guests.

·♥·♥·♥·♥·♥·

As promised, Ethan Donovan arrived just in time for the Secret Santa. He had even brought a gift bag, which he placed with the ever-growing mountain of gifts under the tree. Misty and Lori had done this in previous years, but it seemed like the space under and next to the tree had never been so crowded.

Abundance. Whatever they might be worried about, they had many reasons to be grateful. She would never forget that. Misty's gaze fell on the couple that had taken the last room the night Sabrina arrived. They were standing together, talking. As much as people admired Sabrina, they fortunately observed some boundaries.

Misty wanted the experience to be special for all of them, but most of all for Sabrina. The joy and magic of Christmas was always fleeting, reminding them to be mindful.

She took the small spoon that Lori handed her and clinked it against her glass.

"Merry Christmas everyone!" A chorus of "Merry Christmas" was returned to her. She had to think of the many parties her parents had hosted with friends around the time, for a moment lost in the memory until Lori nudged her. "Okay, as you can see, Santa came last night and has been especially generous. Why don't we open some gifts?"

There was a separate section for children and families just so three-year old Trevor wouldn't find himself with a bottle of brandy. That section came first, also so the few little ones present wouldn't have to wait any longer. Seeing the smiles and happy expressions on everyone's faces, Misty knew that this day could have turned out very differently. She saw Donovan survey the scene with interest.

Maybe this was it. Maybe he had changed his mind and realized that Boxwood worked in ways different from the big city where he worked. After she'd lost her job, and Abby, Misty had been left with many doubts. She wasn't sure if there was a path forward, for herself, for anyone. Injustices and disappointments happened to anyone, and she was aware that hers weren't by far the worst. She still had a roof over her head, she had Lori, her friends...as of now, she still had the business.

And the greatest Christmas surprise ever, Sabrina. For her, this journey was about family first and foremost, rediscovering her roots. It was for Misty, too, thinking back to those perfect Christmases their parents had created for her and Lori. Something to always remember and hold on to.

Lori who sensed her absentmindedness, jumped in to oversee the continuation of Secret Santa. Happy children were already playing with new toys. The guests had moved on to the adult gifts, and the husband of the couple last to arrive this season held up the Brandy with a smile. Other gifts included hand-made items from the Christmas market, scarves and mittens, art, and a few gift cards for businesses around town.

"I see there's something here for Misty," Lori said, holding up the gift bag that Donovan brought.

Her heart skipped a beat. That had to be it. He might want to make a grand gesture in front of an audience, and if it was what Misty hoped, she wouldn't mind.

She caught Sabrina's expression, somewhere between pensive and curious. Once more Misty wondered what she and Emily Davis had to talk about, but that could wait. Smiling at her attentive audience, she removed the paper to find a small box inside. He'd really made it suspenseful. There had to be a reason why Donovan had agreed to come, if his time and money was this precious.

He had to have seen the good that Sabrina's presence had done for Boxwood, whether she'd stay or not. Misty felt a pang of sadness at the latter notion, though for the moment, excitement drowned out everything else.

She opened the box, and her jaw dropped. Eventually, Misty managed to force a smile at the gift card for a boutique out of town. The amount of money was, of course, above the maximum they usually agreed on, a nice sum if you didn't consider the context.

Donovan had never really cared about the inn, and he had no intention of saving it. That became obvious to Misty in a heartbeat.

"Looks like I'm going to have a lovely shopping day," she said, holding up the card. "Thank you for that, Secret Santa. If you'll excuse me? I'll be right back. There's something I need to take care of."

She all but fled from the room, but not before catching the expressions of several people, Sabrina's and Lori's alarmed, Ethan's clueless. Misty headed upstairs to her room where she stood for a few seconds, willing herself not to cry.

Much of it was for sheer exhaustion. First, working so hard to make the season special for their guests when they didn't even know the news that he was going to drop on them. Then, getting all caught up in elevating Christmas in Boxwood to a place where the train still might have a chance, and Donovan wouldn't leave the deal. In between all of this...

Sabrina stepped inside after a quiet knock and pulled her close. Misty gratefully leaned into her embrace. She didn't want to lose it, but she was dangerously close, tears pressing behind her eyes.

"I'm sorry. I'm so sorry. We promised you a great Christmas."

"It's been great so far," Sabrina said softly. "And it's not over yet. I haven't even had the chance to tell you how beautiful you are."

"Thank you. But I'll trust that Lori can wrap things up. I'm done. I'm so tired."

"Look. Misty. It's not over! Donovan was never going to change his mind. Emily and I will buy him out."

Speechless, Misty stepped back and sought Sabrina's gaze, trying to process what she'd just heard. After a few seconds had ticked by, she found words.

"You've got to be kidding me. No, I'm sorry, that came out wrong. How?"

"Let's say we do have some common interests, and I could convince her that it's a worthy cause." Sabrina took both her hands before she sat on the edge of the bed. "But that's not all. We might be able to keep the train running."

"What?" Misty couldn't follow any longer.

"Emily and I had a long conversation, about our goals, the connections we've made and how it all goes together. It turns out that there are things we realized we can do together, and we refuse to let people pit us against one another."

"That is amazing! I...I don't know what to say. Thank you so much."

"We will work out the details, I promise. There's more."

"I'm not sure I'll be able to handle more," Misty admitted.

"It's not bad. Emily got tired of the cat fight stories too, and she's been talking to a few people. We might be able to get something off the ground...It's not exactly the same project I had in mind earlier, but close. It turns out not everyone has forgotten about me."

"That's...so much." Misty wasn't sure she was able to process the news in real time. "That means you'll have to go back to L.A....when?"

"The day after tomorrow," Sabrina said with obvious regret. "But I'll be back as soon as I can, I promise you." Perhaps Misty's doubts had shown in her face because she added, "I mean it. You know it's not just about business, or childhood memories."

"No?" Misty asked as she sat next to her.

"No. They're not even the main reason. You are," Sabrina said as she leaned in to kiss her. Moment by moment, doubts and disappointment fell away. Misty and Abby had lived in the same town, and they couldn't make it work. What mattered wasn't the distance, but the commitment. If she and Sabrina were both willing to make it, they did stand a chance.

She still couldn't believe that Sabrina would have to leave in a matter of days.

A knock on the doorframe startled them apart.

"I just wanted to make sure you're okay, sis...oops." Lori halted her words though walked a few steps into the room. "Come to think of it, you two look very okay, so I'll just pretend I was never here?" she suggested, making all of them laugh.

"We'll be down in a bit," Misty told her. "I hope there's some of that eggnog left, because I'm going to need it, and...by the way, we're not going to lose our business."

"I knew it! Magic, right?"

"Yes. I'll see you *later*."

Lori understood the not-so-subtle nudge and left again.

"We're going to be okay," Misty said. All of it, she and Sabrina, the place and the town they both called home. There was a hint of a question left, but for the most part...She believed.

"Yes. I'll try to be back for New Year's, but if I don't make it, before Valentine's Day for sure. We'll figure something out," Sabrina promised.

"Would you stay with me tonight?" Misty said the words so quickly they almost sounded like one. "I mean, I'm so tired and excited at the same time that I'm not even sure what I'm about to promise, but I want to be close to you." *Before you go,* but Sabrina had understood without her saying it.

"I want that too," she said. "But before that, I want to give you your gift. The Secret Santa was nice, but I wanted you to give you yours in private."

"I had the same idea," Misty admitted, her cheeks still comfortably warm with everything they had exchanged in words, and between the lines.

The gift she had commissioned for Sabrina came from one of the oldest stores in Boxwood.

Sabrina went silent as she unwrapped the ornament in the form of *Misty's Maison Inn.*

"When I got it, I didn't even know what was going to happen, but somehow, I knew Lori and I were going to keep the inn. And that meant you would always have a home here."

"I love it. Thank you so much, Misty." Sabrina embraced her, holding on tightly. When she lifted a strand of Misty's hair, brushing her lips against her neck, Misty nearly forgot about her own gift.

"Later," Sabrina promised. "Now come with me."

In the guestroom, she handed a box to Misty that was surprisingly heavy. The content was every bit as much a surprise as her gift had been to Sabrina.

"That means...You're not giving up on me?"

"Never. I'll be here to teach you, and I promise you, it will be so much fun."

Misty couldn't help laughing, and she hoped Sabrina wouldn't misinterpret her reaction. Because it was so obvious, wasn't it? She'd love everything they'd do together. She was in love, and she couldn't wait to get back on the ice with Sabrina. Even better that it would forever remind her of their first almost kiss...and the real ones that followed. "They're perfect," she added, holding up the shiny new skates. "Just like you."

The night couldn't be any better, could it? Never in her life she had imagined she would make Sabrina Russell blush or thank her for the perfect gift with a tender kiss.

Chapter Fourteen

They went back to the party hand in hand, just in time for another surprise guest showing up.

Mayor Alicia Gaines shook hands and wished people a Merry Christmas before she joined Sabrina and Misty.

"Mayor Gaines, welcome."

"I'm sorry to crash the party, but I won't stay long. I have news. Actually, I think everyone should hear this."

By the time she had finished her sentence, it had gotten quiet around them, as conversations came to a halt, guests sensing that her news might have an impact on the entire town. Misty thought it might be polite to offer her something, but she, too, couldn't handle any more suspense.

"I spoke to the company that runs the train again, and it turns out, they sent a representative to check on our efforts. They brought their two children on the train who loved it so much, their dad wasn't only reminded of his own childhood but had an epiphany."

The mix of hope and excitement in the room was palpable. Misty felt Sabrina grip her hand tighter.

"Well, that, and they saw how much of a success it still is in Boxwood, so they decided to give it another try. It will run for one more year..." Her last words were almost drowned out in cheers. "After that, we'll see, but if we can continue to sell out the tickets...I'm optimistic that it won't be just that one year."

Misty turned to Sabrina, her vision starting to blur with tears of joy. Sabrina pulled her into a brief hug, and then, in front of all the guests and the mayor of Boxwood, she kissed her in a way that was Hollywood-worthy.

When she pulled back, there was applause, leaving Misty red-faced and slightly self-conscious. But it was so worth it.

Their own Christmas miracle had come through.

·♥·♥·♥·♥·♥·

After the party, they started cleaning up before sitting down with a glass of eggnog. Misty could finally fill in Lori on the other rapidly evolving events of the evening.

Sabrina shook her head. "That's just like Ethan, thinking that his gift card makes up for everything. But it's probably a good thing he's out if he was never that interested."

"Yes. And to be fair, it is very generous," Misty admitted, comfortably warm from the eggnog and Sabrina's arm around her.

"You might need to invest in your wardrobe for when you're visiting Sabrina in L.A.," Lori suggested. "It's all working out."

Misty cast an uncertain glance at Sabrina. She knew Lori was joking, but with everything going this fast, they didn't have time to discuss potential future visits. She had seen Emily, and tabloid pictures of the people Sabrina socialized with...

"Don't make that face," Sabrina said. "And Lori, that wasn't nice. Misty's wardrobe is perfect. "I just need to get things started with Emily, and I believe you two are busy running the inn. We'll make time for everything else. I swear."

"You're right. I'm sorry. I'm also happy and grateful at the turn of events. To miracles. Merry Christmas, you two." She raised her glass.

"Merry Christmas," Sabrina and Misty echoed.

***

As predicted, they were both tired and a bit tipsy when they made it to Misty's bedroom, perfectly happy to be close. They'd see each other again soon. Sabrina had mixed feelings about leaving, no matter how exciting the prospects were, but she wouldn't let the emotion take over yet. She wanted to be mindful, enjoy the feel of Misty sleeping in her arms—and take that feeling with her. Eventually, she slipped into slumber, her dreams filled with lights and snowy fields, the sweet taste of hot chocolate...and kissing Misty.

There would be many more kisses...and opportunities.

She might not be able to do everything, but she could still do her part.

She couldn't turn back time, but Sabrina knew she could give the present everything she had, the love for the stories she wanted to tell, and for the woman who had become the center of her own.

Epilogue

DECEMBER 26TH: ONE YEAR LATER

C oming home for Christmas had been the best idea she'd ever had, last year, and now, Sabrina reflected as she and Misty sat cuddling under a blanket as the movie started.

It had been a turbulent and busy year with many blessings for both of them. At the moment, she was grateful they were able to claim that time and space for themselves, just be together.

"I can't believe you're finally here." Misty leaned against her with a happy sigh. "That's my favorite Christmas present."

"Oh, wait until you get my real one."

They had spent Christmas Eve with Lori and had another Secret Santa with the guests of the inn for Christmas Day. A recent storm had turned Boxwood into a winter wonderland, the quiet welcome and so different from the busy city—though Sabrina was grateful for everything it had given her too.

She had to smile at Misty's excitement, because it wasn't her first time watching *For the Taking*. Sabrina would concede that the movie she'd produced and starred in together with Emily Davis was worth watching more than once. An actress her own age had played her love interest in the story about a group of women organizing a heist. It was funny, and thoughtful, and full of action and romance.

Sabrina couldn't have been happier with the result and was proud to show her work when Misty had visited her in L.A. for Thanksgiving...and again this Christmas. She was equally proud of Misty who kept running a successful business. She would have a lot to show for when Emily and her boyfriend, actor Timothy Shepherd, joined them for New Year's Eve to check on Emily's investment.

"I'm so happy for you," Misty commented. "For me, too, obviously, because I love the movie, and it's amazing you got to make it...This was your dream."

"It was." After a box office hit featuring Emily, new opportunities had opened up for Sabrina as well. "I was lucky to make a few others come true along the way."

"Yeah. It's a miracle that the train will be around for a few more years to come."

"It is, but that's not what I meant." Sabrina leaned in to kiss her, momentarily distracting her from the images on the screen.

They might have their challenges, but life was sweet here in Boxwood, Christmas traditions, cookies and...Misty. They'd make the best of every moment.

"I love you," she said.

"I love you too," Misty whispered back.

Sabrina was no longer afraid to look ahead, or sad about the times gone by.

From now on, every Christmas would be merry.

About the Author

B arbara Winkes writes sapphic crime drama and Christmas romance. She loves writing characters who get the job done, whether it's stopping a predator or saving cherished traditions—while still making time for love. She lives with her wife in Quebec City.

barbarawinkes.com

Also by Barbara Winkes

Bells Will Be Ringing
A Girlfriend for Christmas
Christmas Cupid
The Christmas Memory